# Tattered

## A TATTERED HEART DUET #2

USA TODAY BESTSELLING AUTHOR

# BROOKE O'BRIEN

# TATTERED

Maverick Night is bad news. He made me want things I knew I shouldn't but did.

Now my brother's best friend is back, but we are both different people. Time changed us.

I crave the way my heart beat when he used to look at me, how it felt to be in his arms. Nothing good will come from opening myself up to him.

I just hope my tattered heart can take it if he walks away again.

Thank you for reading Tattered, the second installment in the Tattered Heart duet.

You can join my Facebook group, Brooke O'Brien's Rebel Reader Group, to discuss the duet and get sneak peeks on future releases. Sign up for my newsletter to find out more about my new releases. To join, visit

www.authorbrookeobrien.com/follow.
Enjoy the conclusion to Mav and Ryan's story!

# Tattered Heart Duet
## READING ORDER

**TORN**

**TATTERED**

*a brother's best friend, military romance*

Learn more and purchase your copy at:
www.authorbrookeobrien.com/tatteredheartduet

# DEDICATION

This book is dedicated to anyone holding onto hope that love will find its way back to them.

# Prologue

Mav,

Waking up this morning to find you gone has been hard to accept. I keep looking over at where you slept next to me, hoping I'd wake up and this will have all been a dream. You may not have believed in what was between us, but I did. I know how I felt every time you looked at me and kissed me.

I don't know when I'll see you again or if you'll ever come back home to Everton.  Reading your letter, I find myself wanting to hold onto the hope you'll find your way back to me. As long as I have hope, I'll wait for you. I'm going to keep believing in what I felt for you since we first met and hope someday you'll come home to me.

Love,

R

# Chapter One

## MAVERICK
### Four Years Later

It's been years since I've got a full night's sleep. As the days have passed, sleep is starting to feel like a distant memory. The nightmares that plagued me were just a reminder of the hell I was reliving when I was awake. After two tours, one in Iraq and the other in Afghanistan, these nightmares haven't seemed to let up. The only difference now is the monsters chasing me wear a new face.

Life has delivered a bitter pill that I haven't been able to swallow. It's hardened my heart, which when you're in the military, is exactly what you need to serve. If you let shit get you down or get lost in your emotions, you'll end up taking your eyes off the purpose of why you're here.

I know what can happen if you do. You make mistakes, and if you're not careful, you may end up being called home, and I'm not talking in the way you want to be either.

The heat from the humid air is stifling as sweat drips down my forehead. Crossing my arms beneath my head, I adjust the pillow as I close my eyes and enjoy a few minutes of silence.

My platoon and I are about seven months into our time in Kabul, Afghanistan. We're still waiting to hear the official word, but sometime in the next two weeks we should be making our trip back home and fuck if I'm not ready to set foot back on American soil.

"Night, wake up. You got a call."

The loud command bounces off the walls of the tent as I peek my eye open.

James peers his head into the tent. There's a look of surprise on his face as he nods his head toward the tent on the other side of our bunk.

Letters sent to me are few and far between, much less a phone call, so I know, like me, he's wondering what's going on. Once he sees I'm awake, his head disappears again. I wonder who the hell could be trying to get in touch with me.

Stepping out of the tent, my eyes glance at the picnic tables set up outside on the base. Several of the guys are sitting around, playing cards and shootin' the shit. There's not much to pass the time, but you'd be surprised at what you can come up with to keep your mind off what's going on outside the base.

My eyes connect with James standing off to the side. His arms are crossed as he looks on at the other guys playing a game of cards.

"Who is it?"

"No name, but sounded important."

I nod my head. I don't have a good feeling about this and I'd like to get this over with.

Stepping into the Communications Center, I pick up the phone and press the line, connecting the call.

"This is Maverick Night," I state, swallowing down the ball in my throat.

"Mav." It's hard to hear through this phone but I can make out the voice.

"Dean?"

"Yeah, buddy. I'm sorry to call you like this. It took jumping through some hoops to get in touch but listen, your grandmother contacted me yesterday. She was looking for some help in trying to reach you. Got some news for you about your dad."

He pauses for a moment, and I want to tell him to spit it out already. After our fight, I didn't talk to him for several months. When I got back home from basic training, there was a letter from him waiting for me along with one from Ryan. I know Dean holds a lot of regret for the way shit went down. I needed him to know me enlisting wasn't his fault.

Every time I've called him to check in, I fight the urge to ask him what I really want to know. How is Ryan? Is she seeing anyone? Does she miss me as much as I fucking miss her?

"He passed away, man. They're saying his liver failed."

His words rattle around in my head as I replay them over and over.

He is gone.

The mother fucker is actually gone.

I should be surprised at the age of fifty-three, but I know he stopped taking care of himself long before we lost my mom. Her passing away just sped up the process. He started drinking heavier, which led to his anger. I doubt he's even been to the doctor since I left, so any signs or symptoms likely went missed.

"Shit," I mutter, not knowing what to say. "What are the plans then?"

Running my hand over my face, I clench my hand around my jaw as I think of everything that needs to be arranged. The only people my dad had was his brother, Richard, who I don't think he's talked to in over fifteen years and my grandmother. The last thing I want to do is put this on her.

"We're still working it out. I'll help her get everything taken care of, man. No worries, I'll be there. Just let me know what you need."

"I'll figure out how soon I can get out of here. I'll try to give you a call later this evening after I talk to my sergeant."

Dean fills me in on his plan to go with my grandmother to figure out the details. Disconnecting the call, I scrub my hands over my face. I don't even know how I feel hearing the news. There's a part of me that almost feels relieved to know I won't have to face him again.

I walk across the base toward the Command Center, ducking my head as I step inside.

"Sir, do you have a moment?"

I've served the last two tours with Sergeant Jackson. He's grown to be more of a father to me than my own father in a lot of ways. I hold an immense amount of respect for him.

"Of course," he says, setting the papers he was shuffling through down on the table. "Everything alright?"

"I just took a call patched over to me from my friend back home. He wanted to let me know my father passed away yesterday. I was hoping I could talk to you about taking a short leave to help get everything in order."

"I'm sorry to hear about your father," he says.

I want to tell him his sympathy is not necessary, that he doesn't deserve anyone's sadness. Saying that will bring on an onslaught of unwanted questions, so I simply respond with a nod.

"You do what you need to do. We're about to button up things here before we follow you back home, too. Don't bother joining us. We'll see you back home in the States soon."

"That won't be necessary, sir. It should only be a few, three maybe four days at the most, depending on when I get a flight back home. I'd like to come back and finish with the rest of the guys."

"I figured you would say that, but I'll have to decline. We should be heading back shortly after anyway, and it wouldn't serve a purpose to bring you back only to have you return home in a short time. Go home, take care of what you need to, and report to the base when you get everything in order."

I don't press it further.

"I'll see what I can do to arrange you a flight first thing in the morning. Let me know if there is anything I can do before you take off."

Clenching my jaw, I nod my head and lean forward to shake his hand.

As much as I want to help finish things off here, I'm relieved to know my time left in this sandy hell is coming to an end very soon. It isn't until I'm back in my bunk packing that it hits me; this will be the first time in four years I will be back in Everton.

My mind floats back to the phone call with Dean and my thoughts of Ryan. I think about how she looked our last night together, standing outside of her house in the pitch black. Her hair pulled over her shoulder and her boxer shorts rolled at the waist, showing her smooth tan skin on her legs. I hated walking away from her the next morning, I couldn't even work up the courage to say goodbye. I hated knowing I was leaving the only peace I had found since my dad moved us to Everton.

Pulling out the only picture I have of her from my wallet, I sit down on the edge of the mattress. Running my finger along the worn edges, my heart warms looking at her. The edge of her lip is curled, the smirk lining her mouth.

Fuck, I miss her.

The next day was long. I was taken to Germany where I was delivered to the U.S. Army base, then later, boarded a flight bringing me back to the States. When I arrived in Des Moines, I texted Graham to see if he could pick me up from the airport. We had exchanged a few text messages throughout the day, so I knew he had an important meeting about the security company he and Dean were opening.

Feeling tired after all the traveling, I opted to hail a cab and head to the hotel just a few minutes away. The exhaustion was starting to set in, and I was ready to take a much needed nap.

Stepping outside, I'm met with a wall of humidity. Unlike the dry heat I am used to, this heat is completely different. I can feel the perspiration dotting my forehead the moment I step outside. A cab pulls right in front of me, and I send up a silent prayer of thanks it was this easy for me to catch a lift.

Adjusting my duffel bag on my shoulder, I glance down at my phone vibrating in my hand when the door of the cab swings open, hitting me in the arm. The force knocks my cell phone out of my hand and sends it crashing to the ground. My eyes wince as I watch it slide along the hard concrete.

"You really should pay attention to where you're walking."

I could remember that snarky tone anywhere, reminding me of the first day we met. My head jolts in the direction it came from. I'm not able to see her face, but I can tell by the back of her head it's her. She still has the same long, dark hair covered up by her usual backward snapback. She's dressed in her T-shirt, tied at her waist, paired with cut-off denim shorts and Chucks.

My eyes follow her movement as she leans forward to pick up her suitcase, carrying it around to the back of the cab and tossing it into the trunk. I can't help but eat up every inch of her skin. I'm drawn to the ink covering her arm to the dreamcatcher covering her toned thigh.

She looks so much like the girl I remember, but she's different, too.

Leaning over, I grab the back passenger door and hold it open for her, waiting for her to close the trunk and see me. Judging by her comment, I don't know that she realized it was me. There's no way in hell I'm going to let her get away without sharing a cab with her.

When her hands reach up to close the trunk, our eyes connect. Hers widen in shock as her mouth drops open.

"Mav."

My name comes out more of a question, as if asking herself if it's really me. She may look different, but I know I don't look like the same kid she said goodbye to either. My hair is shaved close to my scalp. The tattoos covering my arm are, in a lot of ways, thanks to her. Her artwork growing up inspired a lot of the pieces that are now forever etched into my skin. Her eyes roam over my body, to the duffel bag slung over my shoulder.

Nodding my head, I reply, "Ryan. It's good to see you."

I hold the door open and wave my hand in front of me, encouraging her to climb inside. Her eyes furrow for a moment before she quickly looks up at me. I'm waiting for the inevitable remark to come because when has Ryan ever ignored the opportunity to provide her smart-ass commentary?

"You followin' me around again, Maverick?" Her lip curls up on the edge and I fight off the urge to kiss the smirk right off her sexy mouth.

"Don't tempt me, Rebel." The double meaning is clear. She knows I'd follow her and not do a damn thing to hide it. I also am not even trying to disguise the look of desire on my face.

Pulling her sunglasses from where they are hung on the front of her tank top, she slides them over her face.

"I figured we could share a ride. I'm feeling a little nostalgic after the last time we took a ride together."

"You think you'll be able to keep your hands to yourself this time around?"

I wish I could see her eyes, so I could read her expression. I'm not sure if she's baiting me or if that's what she really wants.

Tilting my head in close to her neck, I let my breath feather across her skin as I whisper, "When I get the chance to put my hands on you again, Rebel, I promise it will be because we both want it. You may even find yourself begging for it."

# Chapter Two

## RYAN

He always loved to rile me up. I'm still trying to wrap my head around the fact he's standing in front of me. In a matter of two minutes, we've slipped back into our comfortable familiarity, as if the last four years and hundreds of miles hadn't separated us.

"Now get in and slide over because I'm riding with you."

Maverick disappears to the back of the cab, pounds his hand on the trunk, waiting for it to pop before climbing in the backseat next to me. He tells the driver to take me wherever I need to go first. After I rattle off the address, he hits the gas like the cops are hot on our heels, and I'm forced to accept Maverick is here, with me in the back of the cab.

I've spent the last four years waiting for the day he came back to Everton. For the first few months after I sent him the letter, I hoped he would change his mind. I spent so many nights crying myself to sleep. I couldn't bring myself to pick up my board again until the night I found out he was deployed to Iraq.

When Dean called me with the news, I raced home and picked up the worn piece of wood and rode down to the river. Until that moment, I couldn't bring myself to go down there. The place held such a special memory of our last night together. Sitting on the edge of the dock, I stared up at the starry night sky and wondered what he was doing and if he was thinking of me, too. The nights when he felt so far away, I found myself back down there just wanting to feel closer to him again.

I feel his eyes on me, burning holes into the side of my face. Being in such a small space together again, you could cut the tension in the air. It's like my body feels the trace of his gaze running over me, and I fight off the urge to turn and ask him why it took him so long to come back.

"How's life been treating you?" he asks, as if reading my thoughts.

Leaning against the car door, I glance over at Mav and let my eyes rake over his body. It's hard not to stare at him. He's changed so much since we last saw each other. He was always muscular; years of skating and working out left his body chiseled in all the right places. He's different now though.

He doesn't attempt to shy away from the way my eyes burn into him the same way his did mine. It's been too long since I had him next to me, so I let my eyes drink him in.

"It's been forever since I last saw you. I guess when I think about how long ago that was, it feels like so much has changed. I thought you were still overseas?"

It's my attempt to change the subject, divert the attention off me. Maybe it's a wall up or maybe I'm more curious about him, but I want to know why he's back in Everton after so many years without a single word.

His eyebrows knit together at the mention of him being overseas. It's almost like he's surprised I've kept up with his whereabouts over the years. It's not hard when I know he stays in touch with my brother. As much as Dean condemned us for our relationship back then, he knows how much I still care about Mav.

"Yet here I am," he says.

It doesn't escape me he's steered the conversation away from my question. The statement hangs in the air before I reply, "Yet here you are."

Peering out the window, I watch as the buildings in downtown Des Moines pass us by. The wind flows through the backseat, causing strands of my hair to whip around my face covering part of my mouth. I don't bother moving them, turning my baseball cap around to shield my eyes.

"It's good to see you finally got your ink."

The mention of the tattoos covering my arms and legs bring back a swarm of memories of the first night we spent alone together. The night I opened up to him about the ink that covered my skin and, when he shared with me, all the reasons why he found himself knocking on Dean's bedroom window at night.

The cab pulls up in front of the tattoo shop and I watch as Maverick looks past me, out the window to the building behind me. His eyes narrow for a moment before turning back to me. Something that looks like a smile plays at the corner of his mouth. He doesn't say anything, doesn't even attempt to acknowledge the tattoo shop but I can see the pride he wears on his face. Despite all these years, the feelings and the way things were left, he's proud of me for how far we've come.

Reaching my hand over, I pull the lever to the door and move to step out.

"Here, let me help you with that," he mutters, swinging his door open and jumping out. The driver pops the trunk, and before I know it, Maverick is quickly pulling my suitcase out and setting it on the ground between us.

There's so much I want to ask him, to have him sit down and tell me, but things are different now. I was just a chapter in his book, one that was never meant to be re-read. It's become very apparent over the years after he never responded to my letter.

I just never expected that it would be four years before I would see or hear from him again. Maybe I'm feeling a little sentimental after seeing him again, but I can't help but feel like we are miles apart.

"Well, this is me," I say, pointing to the front of Tattered, the tattoo shop I own with my buddy, Chris. "It's good to see you, Mav. It's even better to know you're here, that you're home and safe." The thought of him being over there, fighting a war, is something that was never far from my mind.

"It's good to see you, too, Rebel. I never thought I'd be back here, but it's good to be home."

I feel as if there is more to his comment he's not telling me, but I decide not to push it. It's not my place to go asking questions I have no business asking.

"I'll be in town for a little bit. I'd like to get together, maybe we can grab lunch and catch up?"

"As much as I've waited for you to be home and to hear those words, a lot has changed. I have changed. I think it's best if we leave the past in the past," I reply, swallowing hard. I hate even saying those words. "Take care of yourself, Mav," I reply, flashing him a small smile as I grab the handle of my suitcase and force my feet to move.

I hear him mutter a goodbye as I pass him, but I don't turn around to see the look on his face.

It's time I accept his place in my life and in the past. Not because I don't care about him, but because it's better to leave all the things unsaid and where they are meant to be.

The door dings as I pull it open. Andi steps out of the back room with a box in her hands, peeking her eyes around the corner to see who it is.

"Hey, I was wondering when you'd be back."

Chris rolls his chair backward from where he works when he realizes it's me.

"About fucking time!" he shouts.

My day has been non-stop since I woke up early this morning to catch my flight home from California. I had planned on stopping by Tattered knowing I have a busy week ahead catching up on appointments I had to reschedule around my trip, on top of working at the bar this weekend with Nadia.

My thoughts are still caught up in what just happened that it takes me a minute to catch up.

Flashing Chris my middle finger, I saunter into my room on the other side of the shop, just needing a moment to collect myself. My heart feels like it's beating again for the first time since I last saw Maverick, and it's terrifying.

# Chapter Three

## MAVERICK

My body was starting to wear down. I was glad when the cab pulled up in front of the hotel because I felt like I was riding a high after seeing Ryan, but it all came crashing down when she said her goodbyes and I was forced to watch her walk away from me.

Graham texted me on my way to the hotel asking to meet up later tonight for a drink at the local bar, Champions. A nap was in order if there was any chance of me doing that. My alarm clock goes off, and I slide my hand under my pillow, grabbing my phone. Holding it in front of me, I peek one eye open and turn off the alarm before pulling the pillow over my head.

It feels like only a few seconds pass when the phone starts ringing. Groaning, I don't bother checking the screen as I swipe to answer.

"'Lo."

"You alright over there, man?" Graham's husky voice filters through the phone.

"I'm getting up right now. This jet lag is killin' me."

"I hear ya. I'm just getting home from dealing with all sorts of bullshit today. I'm going to hop in the shower quick. You think you'll be ready in about twenty minutes?"

"Yeah, man, I'll see ya there."

We disconnect the call and I finally pull myself out of bed. I quickly put in a request for an Uber to pick me up. I splash some water on my face and brush my teeth before throwing on a change of clothes. We pull up a little early since the bar is close and it only takes a few minutes to get there.

Heading inside, I bypass the server station and make a beeline directly to the bar. I know Graham will be here any minute, and I'm not wasting any time to put in my order for a beer.

A few minutes later, just as I take a long pull from my beer, I feel a clap on my back, taking me off guard and causing me to nearly choke. Turning my head, I see a rare smirk grace Graham's face. After catching my breath and forcing out a cough, I hold up my middle finger before I stand to give him a hug.

After all the shit I've witnessed overseas, it feels real fucking good to see someone who reminds me of happier times. Growing up, Graham was always a dare devil, Dean was the rowdy one, and I was usually the mellow voice of reason that went along for the ride.

A lot of things have changed with Graham since we were both together in Everton. The paths our lives have led us down have forced us to evaluate where we were going. Graham isn't the same person he was back then; life has shaped him in a different way.

"Good to see you, man. Glad to have you back home. I hope this means you're stayin' for good."

"It's good to be home."

I see his eyebrow rise, as if he is waiting to hear if I'll be staying in Everton. The answer is I'm not sure where I'm going now that I'm here. I hadn't given it much thought but after seeing Ryan today, I would be lying if I said I hadn't considered staying and spending more time with her.

"Speaking of being home, I thought you were still livin' in Chicago. What made you decide to plant roots back here?"

After I left and moved in with my Aunt Patricia, we all started going down different paths. Graham and Dean have stayed close friends, but I know the drinking picked up after I left. Things started to spiral, especially after Graham lost his cousin, Gage. After graduation, he took off for Chicago and vehemently denied coming back home.

"Yeah, my mom hasn't been doing so well. The doctors were concerned when her health took a turn. She was in the hospital a couple months ago. I decided it was time I came back and look after her."

"I'm sorry to hear about your mom, man. I am sure she's glad to have you back though. It sounds like things are going well with the business, too. I'm happy for you and Dean."

"Thanks. He's staying back in Chicago for now, but the plan is to open two locations for Compass Security. He'll run the operations in Chicago and I'll oversee things from our office in

Everton. I swear though, it's been one thing after another this past week."

"I can imagine it's not easy but I'm sure it will all work itself out."

He grunts in response, nodding his head. He raises his hand, flagging down the waitress.

I almost wouldn't recognize her right away until her eyes and mischievous smile light up her face.

"Nadia," I say in greeting.

"If it isn't the bad boy himself," Nadia retorts as she pulls two glass bottles out of the cooler. Popping the tops, she slides them along the counter toward us.

I'm reminded just how small Everton really is, after only being here for a day.

"Something like that," I drawl, taking a pull from the beer as she leans forward to take my empty bottle. I need to slow it down. It's been awhile since I've drank, and they are going down like water.

I watch as Nadia flashes me a wink as she turns and struts into the back room.

Focusing my attention back to Graham, we continue to chat about how things are going with the business, his move back home, and my dad's funeral.

"How long are you planning on staying in town?"

"Honestly, I haven't thought that far ahead. I never expected to come back here though either."

"I hear ya there, man. I'll be doing some hiring. I will need some help in getting shit up and running. If you end up deciding to stick around, give it some thought. I could use you and your experience."

The job would be perfect, honestly. I haven't considered what I will do when I get out of the army but this sounds right up my alley.

I promise to give it some thought and let him know when I figure out my plans. I know I'll be sticking around for a little bit. I need to sort out what I'm going to do with my dad's stuff. The house will need to be put on the market, because regardless of whether I am staying or going, I refuse to live in his house.

"I'm going to take a leak. I'll be right back." I really want to take a break from this conversation.

Sliding off the barstool, I round the end of the bar toward the long narrow hallway. Nearing the end of the bar, I'm surprised when I look up and see Ryan walk out of the back room

I just saw Nadia disappear to. The second my eyes connect with hers, the wink Nadia gave me earlier makes sense.

"You're followin' me again."

"Wouldn't you love that, Rebel?" I joke, approaching her.

She leans against the wall. "Dream on."

I can't control the laugh at that point. She looks so fucking good now. She changed her clothes from when I last saw her. By the way her eyes rake over my body, she's appreciating the change in my clothes as well. My eyes travel to the edge of her tank top, down to the exposed skin on her arm.

It's as if my feet move on their own accord, taking me closer to her. I have no control over the pull between us. The urge to take in the ink covering her tan skin is too strong.

Our close proximity takes her off guard as I move to survey her tattoos. As soon as my eyes take in the vines covering her shoulder to the heart on her forearm, I feel like my heart is beating so hard it could pound damn near out of my chest. I recognize the heart etched permanently on her skin.

"Ryan," I mutter close to her ear. She must be able to hear the question in my tone, as she moves to pull her hair over her other shoulder, giving me full access to her arm. Her throat bobs with her deep swallow before she turns her head up to peer at me.

I can't help it; I reach my hand out and run my thumb over her skin to the tattered heart etched on her skin. I take in the intricate design, the barbwire and stitching holding it together. You'd think this was the first time I saw the artwork, but it's not. I've stared at it many times, but never with her as the canvas.

"I can't believe you…" I pause, not sure where I'm going with what I'm about to say next. My eyes travel up her arm to meet her eyes. I can see the hint of pain, but she quickly covers it up, locking her hard expression on her face. Her jaw clenches, holding back all the words she wants to say.

Leaning forward, I press a soft kiss against her skin. The action forces Ryan to take a step backward, only to push her back against the wall. I know I shouldn't have done that, but I couldn't help it.

"Will you tell me what this tattoo means to you, Ryan?"

I know she would never put something on her body permanently if it didn't have meaning to it.

"It's my reminder to be protective of your heart and to be careful who you give it to."

"You don't have to protect your heart around me. It's been four years, Ryan, but there hasn't been a single day that went by where I didn't think about you. There wasn't a minute when my body didn't ache for you."

"Why are you here?"

My eyebrows knit together. "I met up with Graham."

"No—" she cuts me off. "I'm talking here, as in Everton. What are you doing here?"

"I got a call two days ago that my dad passed away. I came home for the funeral."

Her throat moves as she swallows down whatever she was going to say next, obviously not expecting that as my response.

"Ryan," I say before she holds her hand up stopping me.

"This can't happen between us again. I can't have you pushing your way back into my life."

"Pushing my way? Is that really what you think I'm doing?" My body goes rigid.

"Isn't it? You take what you want and then you flee. I'm not going to let you do that to me again." She leans away from me, crossing her arms over her chest.

"Rebel, I may not have come back here for the sole purpose of getting you back, but if there was ever a reason I would stay, it would be for you."

I hadn't even thought about it until the words were out of my mouth, but I knew they were true with absolute certainty. I know there's a lot of history between us, history she's obviously still hurting over. That won't stop me from trying to make it right. She's all I ever wanted and I've spent every day of the last four years missing her.

"You can't come back here, force yourself on me, and expect me to just forgive you. That isn't how this works."

"Force myself on you? Is that what you think this is?"

She hesitates for a minute, as I take a step closer, crowding her space. I can hear the stutter around the inhale of her breath. Her chest heaves, and I can't help the smile lining the edge of my mouth.

"You can't try and tell me you don't feel this between us, Ryan. It's still there." I lean in closer, my breath feathering along the edge of her lips. "My body still aches for you after all these years. I said this to you earlier and I meant every fucking word. I will have you begging for it, because trust me baby you can try and deny it all you want, but I know your sweet pussy aches for me, too."

"Shit," she mutters as her eyes glaze over. Her head tilts back as her struggled breaths float over my skin warming me further.

"Tell me you want me to touch you and I will."

"No—" she demands, clenching her jaw.

Leaning forward, I blow softly along the nape of her neck up toward her ear before I continue. "You've always been a shit liar, Rebel. I can smell the arousal on you, baby. I can tell by the way your skin flushes, the subtle way you are clenching your legs together, to the way you are forcing yourself to breathe. Do you think I could make you come just standing here without even touching you?"

Her head rears back as she looks up at me as if I'm crazy. The sinister smile I greet her with says just how much I'd love for her to challenge me.

"Mav," she stutters. The desire overtakes her, causing her resolve to slip away.

"Or do you want me to touch you?"

Her eyelids lower. The desire winning out. "Say it," I whisper encouragingly.

"I want—" she swallows before forcing herself to continue, "I want you to touch me."

Grunting, I wrap my arm around her and pull her closer to me.

I can tell by the look in her eyes she knows I'm talking somewhere close and quick because my patience is wearing thin.

Pulling me around the corner, she opens the door to what looks like a small supply closet and quickly pulls me inside. I don't have time to look around before the door shuts behind us. This is the last place I want our reunion to be, but I just need a minute with her, alone.

Pushing her up against the door, her hands wrap around the waistband of my jeans, and she pulls me closer. Her fingers skate along the edge of my boxer briefs and my aching cock strains against my zipper.

Easing my hand around her waist, I bring her closer to me. I'm so thankful for the short-shorts and tank top she's wearing. She has given me easy access to all the parts of her body I've missed the most.

Sliding my hands over the curve of her ass, I pull her closer, easing my hand beneath the edge of her tank top, along the smooth skin of her back, and up the curve of her spine.

"Maverick," she whispers, running her hand along the buzzed hair along the back of my head, pulling me closer to her. As soon as our mouths connect, I can't help but unleash a groan from deep in my throat, vibrating against her mouth.

When her tongue traces a line along the edge of my mouth, I know I'm fucking done for. This girl has been featured in all my fantasies while I was gone. She's all I have been able to think about since I left her, and it doesn't hardly seem real she's standing right here in front of me, in my arms.

"Rebel," I groan. "You're fuckin' killin' me here."

I didn't want the first time we are together again to be like this.

"Baby, it's going to kill me to say this but when I finally have those sexy as sin legs around me again, I don't want it to be in some dirty supply closet. I want it to be in a bed where I can enjoy having you all to myself."

Even in the darkness, I'm able to make out the look of arousal on her face. "What time are you off?"

"After eleven."

I know it was around eight when we got here so I'm likely going to be carrying a fucking brick in my pants until she is off.

"I'll be waiting for you. Eleven o'clock comes and you're mine."

# Chapter Four

## RYAN

Holy shit. What just happened?

I've been waiting for what has felt like forever to see Maverick again. It's crazy how much can change in a matter of twelve hours.

After Maverick told me he'd be waiting, he opened the door and strutted out of the back room like nothing had just happened. I'm usually able to keep my cool, not much is able to break this hard exterior I usually keep locked in place like a fortress.

That has all gone out the window since Maverick walked back into my life. Pulling my hat off my head, I run my hands through my hair and press the back of my hand against my mouth, trying to gain some semblance of control. The attraction I've always felt for Maverick hasn't gone away, even after all this time.

I open the door and walk back out into the bar, heat rising beneath my skin, thinking back to how Maverick had me pressed against the door. His hardness rubbing against my aching center, full of promise of what's to come later tonight.

As soon as I near the bar, Nadia appears out of nowhere from the back room and pulls me by the arm behind her. My eyes flutter around the room and land on Maverick, where he's seated at the bar. There's a knowing smirk on his face as he tips the bottle of Bud Light toward me before taking a long pull.

"What the hell just happened?" Nadia asks, taking the words out of my mouth from just a moment ago.

"What are you talking about?" I question, playing coy. I know it's stupid considering half the bar likely saw him press me against the wall before I dragged him down the hallway to the supply closet.

I wasn't even paying attention to what was going on around me, or even who may have been watching us. I had been so caught up in the moment it was like nothing else existed.

"Don't play those games with me, Ry. I just saw how you two were grinding against each other, right in the middle of the bar might I add. Then, all the sudden I turn around and you're gone."

"We were just talking. It's not a big deal." I roll my eyes, exasperated.

"Talking, huh? Is that what they call it now? Were you talking about all the ways he'd like to fuck you because that's what it looked like to me."

I nearly choke on air, causing me to spiral in a fit of coughs. My eyes furrow at Nadia and the smug as fuck grin on her face says it all.

"You're a crude one there, Nad."

"You love me for it."

Shaking my head, I turn to push the door open and saunter back into the bar but not before she yells behind me, "This is not the end of this conversation, Ryan Marie. I want the details and you better fucking spill them."

The night creeps by at a snail's pace after that. Maverick and Graham sit at the end of the bar, shooting the shit and every second that ticks by, I can sense his eyes on me. Undressing me.

Sauntering over to where they are seated, I see that Mav is running low, so I pull another beer out of the cooler and pop the cap before sliding it over to him.

"Trying to get me drunk?" Maverick asks, raising his eyebrow. He flashes me a wink before he swallows what's left of his beer and sets the bottle on the counter.

"I know you're a sure thing, Night. No need to get you drunk to have my way with you."

Graham laughs. He looks like he's good on his beer, so I turn to check on the other bar patrons.

The rest of the night tends to flow just like that. A couple of Graham's friends come in later. I don't know them well, but I've seen them around town. I smile at their warm welcome home and give Maverick some time with his friends.

"You can take off now if you want. It's not super busy tonight so we should be able to cover it while you're gone," Nadia says, taking the empty bottle of vodka from my hand.

"You sure? I only have about twenty minutes left before I'm off."

"I'm sure. I've seen the way he's been eye-fucking you all night. The poor guy needs to be put out of his misery. Call me tomorrow because I want the details. I mean, all of them," she says, pointing the bottle at me as she raises her eyebrows, making sure I know she's serious.

Nadia was there for me through all the heartache after Maverick left town. I understand why he left; I do. It doesn't make the fact it ended before we ever got started hurt any less. We were both in two different places in our lives and I know he didn't want to drag me down the path he was going on when who knows if it would've ever worked.

Printing out their tab, I walk over to where Maverick and Graham are sitting and slide the bill toward them.

"We're not quite ready yet," Maverick says. The hint of laughter plays on his lips.

"Yes, you are, Private Night. It turns out I'm off early and we have plans, remember?"

"Oh, I remember alright. How could I forget?"

The sound of Graham chuckling registers in my mind but I don't even care. This is just the first round of foreplay and I'm not about to miss out.

"Hurry up, then. I'm starting to get impatient and I feel like I've waited long enough."

He grunts before tipping the bottle of beer taking a long pull before slamming the remaining contents down on the bar.

"Sorry, man. I got plans and gotta take off. I'll see you tomorrow." He grins, never taking his eyes off me.

Graham raises his beer to him before flashing me a knowing smirk. My face warms and he must be able to read my expression as he winks and drinks it down. Standing off to the side of the bar near the employee entrance, I wave at Nadia while I wait for Maverick to say his goodbyes.

His shoulders are tense as his muscular legs eat up the distance between us, approaching me. He doesn't stop until his arm is wrapped around my lower back, ushering me out the door.

"You're going to have to drive. I took an Uber here and I'm not in any condition to be behind the wheel."

Reaching into my back pocket, I pull out the remote to my Jeep and press the unlock button. Maverick leads me over to the driver's side door. Before opening the door, he cages me in against the side of the SUV and leans in, kissing me.

My hand wraps around the base of his neck, pulling him in closer to me. His tongue skates along my bottom lip as his hands clench my hips. I feel him against my stomach as he mutters a quiet "shit", his body rocking against me.

He tilts his head back and whispers, "You better make this a quick drive or I'm not sure I'll make it. I'm fucking dying to be inside of you."

My eyelids lower at his words as I tilt my head back against the door.

"Then we should probably hurry."

He moves to step back, opening the door for me and helping me inside. Turning the key in the ignition, the music blares to life. The sound of *Saving Abel* blares through the speakers as I gaze over at Maverick. The grin that takes over his face is filled with so much pride hearing the lyrics.

My tongue skates along my lower lip, wetting my dry skin, as I put the Jeep in reverse and back out. Maverick's hands are all over me as I drive. His hand resting on my thigh is making me crazy, to the point I'm having a hard time focusing on anything but the feel of his rough calloused skin on me. My thoughts play back the first and only time we've been together.

I let myself think about who else he could've been with over the years before I quickly push it out of my mind. I've dated while he's been gone. I never expected for him to find his way back here, never expected for us to be together like this again.

None of the other guys have ever made me feel even a small fraction of what I felt when we were together. Pulling up along the side of Tattered, confusion lines Maverick's features.

"I own the entire building. The upstairs is a loft apartment and the downstairs is our tattoo shop."

Sliding out of the Jeep, we climb the stairs on the outside of the building leading to the balcony on the side. Standing in front of the door, Maverick's hands wrap around my waist, pulling me in close. His cock is resting against the curve of my ass as he pulls my hair off the nape of my neck.

"I've missed you," he whispers, his tongue tracing the shell of my ear, causing my skin to pebble and a chill to run down my spine. "It's been awhile so I'm sorry if this first time is over quick, but I promise I'll make it up to you."

My earlier fear over how many women he's been with is quickly tamped down. I know I can't be bothered by him moving on. He's a man and he has needs, but the thought of him fulfilling them with someone else makes my heart ache.

I don't know how long he's planning on being in town or when he is leaving again, so I tell myself to push all those negative thoughts aside and just enjoy the feel of being in his arms again. Even if it's for tonight, if this is all I can have, I will make the most of it.

My hands fumble, but I finally slide the key in the lock and open the door. Maverick's body is pressed behind me, urging me to hurry before the door is slammed shut behind us. The light above the oven in the kitchen is on, adding just enough light.

My back is pushed against the hard door and his body is once again on mine. Our hands and mouths are everywhere. Maverick's hands clench the hem of my tank top before quickly whipping it over my head and tossing it somewhere behind him. His mouth is on me, tracing a line of kisses down my chest and over my stomach. Kneeling on the floor before me, he peers up at me. His long eyelashes combined with the lust on his face makes his gray eyes look even more beautiful.

He makes quick work of unbuttoning my shorts. The material quickly falls to the floor around my ankles. The ink covering my left thigh is fully on display for him now and his eyes skate over the design, trying to take it in. I know he's searching for the hidden meaning before his eyes bounce back up to mine.

Biting my lip, I run my hand over his short hair. The prickly hairs adding friction to the soft skin on the palms of my hand. Wrapping the palms of my hands around his face, I bend forward and press a punishing kiss against his lips. Maverick lets out a deep groan as his hands clasp around my waist.

His mouth tears away from mine as he huskily commands, "Lean back, baby. I need to see you."

I do as he says because the way the words pass his lips, I know he means it. Normally I would love pushing his buttons, but this is a side of Maverick I haven't seen a lot of, but I fuckin' love it. I want more of it. I want more of him and everything he's prepared to give me.

He leans forward and presses a kiss to the ink covering my skin, trailing kisses up my leg to the apex of my thigh. His heated breath through the lace of my panties makes it difficult to stay on my feet, but I am not anywhere near prepared for what he is about to do next.

His tongue darts out and runs along my slit. Even through the fabric of my underwear, it is just enough to drive me wild.

"Fuck," Maverick hums, tilting his head back to look at me. Running my hand back over the top of his head, I pull him closer to me again, earning me another hum of approval. His tongue runs over my pussy and my legs feel as though they could give out at any second.

"You taste as sweet as I imagined, Rebel. Like heaven and hell and everything I shouldn't want, but I do." Running his palms up my thighs, he pulls my underwear to the side and moves my leg over his shoulder. The move positions him up close and personal with my clit and he wastes no time getting down to business.

His tongue darts out, running over my sensitive bud. My body seeks him out, wanting more as I grind against his face. His hands hold my hips, guiding my movements, and it isn't long before I feel my release racing through me.

Holding his head against my pussy, muffling his moans, I start chanting over and over not to stop. I'm teetering on the edge of my release when his mouth clamps around my clit, sucking. My leg threatens to give out when Maverick's strong arm holds me up as the aftershocks race through my body.

When he's confident I can stand on my own, he moves my leg over so I'm standing in front of him. Rolling my head forward, I look down at him and find him with a smug grin on his face. The evidence of my arousal is left on his mouth as his tongue darts out and licks his lips.

I don't even care at this point as I lean forward and kiss him deeply, my fingernails dragging against the skin at the base of his neck. The guttural moan he unleashes fills me with a deep satisfaction.

"Now it's my turn, Rebel. That sweet as fuck mouth has brought me to my knees before. It's time I feel it around my cock."

# Chapter Five

## MAVERICK

There's a heated look on Ryan's face hearing my dirty talking. Fuck, this girl is perfect. So fucking perfect for me.

Moving to stand up in front of her, I wrap my hands around her waist and pull her closer to me, pressing a kiss against her lips before tugging her by the arm with me.

For the first time since stepping into Ryan's loft, I let my eyes take in her space. It's everything I would expect in her home. She has a small living room with a kitchen off to the side. She doesn't have a lot of furniture, just a small high-top table and a loveseat facing the wall-mounted television. Off to the side, taking up most of the space, is an easel and a desk. Papers litter the table top and I can see this is where she likely spends most of her time. I picture her sitting there for hours, drawing.

Looking over my shoulder at her, my eyes connect with hers and I find her watching me take in her home. I've always found myself looking for the hidden meaning, little tidbits of information that cue me in to who she is or what she's thinking.

Running the palm of her hand over my forearm, she pulls me closer and presses a soft kiss against my mouth again. It's as if she can read my thoughts; I only hope she knows how much it means to me to be here. To soak up any time with her I can.

"Let's go upstairs," she whispers against my mouth before feathering another soft kiss against my lips. Nodding my head, I let her pull me behind her.

Not many women I know feel as comfortable in their skin as Ryan does. Standing in front of me in her black lace thong underwear and bra, she leads me across her apartment and up the stairs into the loft.

As soon as we take the final step, I don't waste any time. We've never been alone like this before, where there is no one threatening to interrupt us. Wrapping my hands around her hips, I step up close to her, moving her so she's standing at the foot of her bed.

Rubbing my dick against the curve of her ass, it strains against my zipper, begging to break free. Ryan's soft hand reaches behind her and wraps around the front of my jeans. Squeezing my eyes shut, I moan into her ear, "Easy, baby. When I cum, I plan to be inside you. I don't care if it's in your mouth or in your pussy, I'll let you choose."

Leaving the invitation hanging in the air, she wastes no time to make her decision as she slowly lowers herself to her knees, kneeling before me. Her hands make quick work to unzip my pants and pull them down my legs. They only make it about halfway down my thighs when she pulls on the belt, sliding it through the hoops.

She moves to stand, the salacious grin that stretches out across her face has me raising my eyebrow.

"Hold your hands out, Mav."

My lip curves up, knowing where she's going with this.

"Rebel," I taunt.

"You're not going anywhere this time around. Hold your hands out."

Letting out a deep chuckle, I hold my hands together in front of me and watch as she wraps the leather belt around my wrists. The buckle tightens, biting into my skin as she peeks up at me. I'm not about to tell her it's too tight.

Pieces of her hair fall over her breasts, distracting me from the way her hands work.

Holding my hands against my chest, I lean my head toward her and feel her shallow breaths against the curve of my neck. Her small hand runs along the planes of my chest while the other wraps tightly around the base of my dick.

"I promise, before the night is over, you'll remember who you have belonged to for all these years."

She slides down to her knees once again, leaning forward and swipes her tongue over the head of my cock. She hums softly in appreciation as she licks the bead of pre-cum before taking me in her mouth.

My hips jolt forward on their own accord, taking her off guard but she quickly recovers.

Grabbing onto my thighs, she urges my body toward her. The sounds of her moans fill the air as she continues to bring me closer to her.

"Fuck, that feels so good," I grit out, watching as my dick tunnels in and out of her mouth.

Reaching down, I wrap my hand around her fist, holding off my release. "I changed my mind, baby. I want to cum in your pussy. Stand up," I command.

She moves to stand and doesn't wait for another word as she pushes me down, sitting on the edge of the mattress.

Wrapping my hand around my aching cock, I pump my hand up and down as she moves to stand in front of me, sliding the lacy material down her legs until it falls on the floor. She leans forward, pushing me forcefully on the chest so that I recline back.

Moving to climb over the top of me, she positions herself above me as I move my restrained hands behind my head. She rubs the head of my cock along her folds, lining the head up and leaning back onto her haunches.

I'm not sure what I expected this to feel like after all this time, as she slowly takes my dick until I bottom out. She doesn't move as I tilt my hips up, making a rotating movement. I'm scared if she moves to pull out, I'm going to cum, ending this before we have a chance to get started.

Forcing my eyes shut, I let out a deep breath as I tilt my head up toward the ceiling. I'm searching for some sense of control because this woman is going to ruin me.

"Gimme a sec. You're so tight, so hot, and so fucking perfect. Just give me a fuckin' second."

I feel her hand reach down, rubbing her fingertips over her pussy seeking her own release. The movement causes her pussy to clench like a vise around my dick.

"Holy shit," I mutter as she raises up and forces her body back down against me.

"Oh, god, Maverick. That feels so good," she mutters as her head falls back. Her cries filter through the air as I raise my hips up meeting her thrust for thrust. Now that we've been together, now that I've had a taste of her again, I don't know if I'll be able to look back.

"I'm going to come," she moans. Her fingers resume their strumming on her clit, causing her pussy to tighten around me.

"Shit," I sputter, unable to hold back anymore. With one, two more thrusts I slam into her a third time and unleash a deep moan as my release follows right behind it.

Ryan collapses onto my chest. Holding my hands up, she unbuckles the belt and eases it off my wrists and onto the floor before she wraps her arms around me. She looks so beautiful, almost peaceful like this. The thought of her falling asleep on my chest has memories from the first night I stayed with her in her room floating back through my mind.

The sound of an alarm clock blaring in the distance rustles me from my sleep as I peek one eye open just as Ryan is rolling out of bed. Still dressed in her bra, she stumbles across the room and down the stairs, leaving only the sound of her soft footsteps in her wake.

A few minutes later, I hear her pad across the hardwood floor as she rounds the end of the bed with her cell phone in hand.

Adjusting the pillow under my arm, I gaze up at her as she takes a seat on the edge of the bed.

"It's after nine in the morning," she states as she turns her head toward me. "I'm not sure if you have anywhere to be, but I can give you a ride if you want. I don't have to be at the shop until noon, so we have some time."

"That works. I have to be at the funeral home around eleven-thirty. If you want to drop me off at my hotel room, that would be great."

"How are you doing with everything? I'm sure it can't be easy knowing he's gone."

"Please," I sigh, knowing my father doesn't deserve an ounce of sympathy. "You know how I feel about that asshole. Nothing has changed. Except now I don't have to put up with him, not that I did to begin with."

"I know you didn't see eye to eye, but he's still your dad."

Her eyes roam over my face, looking for any sign I'm not being truthful.

"He was anything but a dad to me. Anyway, I'm going to meet with the minister today. Thankfully, he left behind a will so most of his last wishes were outlined there. I just have to get all of the shit handled. I'll likely be in town for a little bit, at least to figure out cleaning out his house and get it up for sale."

Nodding her head, she looks at me before glancing back down at her phone. I know based on our conversation she wasn't expecting me to stay, but I also know by the look on her face she wasn't prepared for me to leave either.

"I'd like to spend some time together while I am here, if that's alright with you."

I can see the thoughts swirling around in her head before her eyes meet mine.

"I'd like that." She smiles as I reach for her hand. She studies our fingers as they wrap together before looking back up to meet my eyes. "I'm sorry; if I didn't already have appointments booked, I'd come with you. Give you a hand and help you with anything I could. You shouldn't have to go through all of this alone."

Sitting up, I let the sheet fall away covering only my bottom half as I wrap my hand in Ryan's hair, pulling her closer to me. Pressing my mouth against hers, I do my best to avoid the topic of my dad and focus on being here with her. She's always been able to give me peace when my thoughts get to be too loud.

***

I feel relieved after I get all the arrangements made at the funeral home. After I leave, I catch an Uber and get dropped off at Compass Security. Walking along the sidewalk toward the front door, I can see Graham pacing the floor with the phone pressed against his ear.

The doorbell rings when I swing the glass door open.

"Well, that's not fucking good enough. We need to lock in this account. It's huge for us, considering the opening is less than a week away."

Turning to face me, he holds up a finger before marching toward the back of the room and into his office. Giving him a minute to finish up the phone call, I take a seat on the couch in the lobby area. With my arm draped across the back of the cushion, I look around the room to the art hanging on the wall.

It's been less than two months since Graham moved back to Iowa and he's accomplished a lot in a short time, kicking off the opening of his security business in Des Moines. I'm completely blown away by what he's accomplished.

My phone vibrates in my pocket. Reaching in, I pull it out and quickly unlock the screen. I'm so absorbed in a text message from Ryan thanking me for how tired she feels this morning that I don't even bother paying attention as the doorbell dings again until his voice rings through the room.

"Well, I'll be fucking damned. Look who it is." The husky voice has my lip curving up in a small smile.

Hitting send on my text, I slide my phone back in my pocket and move to stand. Holding my hand out in front of me, I'd be lying if I didn't say it was good to see Dean again.

A lot has changed between us since the last time I stood before him. He still looks just like he did that night, except for the change in his build. He's obviously changed his workout, adding a lot of bulk and muscle to him than what he had when we were eighteen.

"Here you thought you ran me out of town," I joke, winking at him.

"Fuck you," he retorts as I let out a laugh.

Pulling me closer, he claps me on the back in a hug as he mutters how it's good to see me in my ear.

Leaning back, he widens his stance as he crosses his arms in front of him.

"It's good to see you back. You plannin' on staying long?"

"He's not going anywhere, I'm giving him a job," Graham says from behind me as I turn to face him. My eyes narrow, knowing now he's mentioned it in front of Dean, I'm going to have the two of them hounding me until I agree.

"Really? Man, that's great!"

I shake my head at Graham and the small smile playing at the corner of his mouth.

"Yeah, I don't know about that. I'm due back on the base after I get everything in order. I'm not sure where I'm going from here."

Dean's hand wraps around his jaw, pausing as he tries to read me. It's no use, I'm a closed book.

"Well, it's good to have you home. You should stay; I know Ryan will be happy to see you, too."

Graham passes by Dean, walking around to the other side of the lobby.  He glances at me over Dean's shoulder, knowing that I've already been reacquainted with his sister for the first time in years. The rare grin that stretches on his face has me silently telling him to fuck off, which earns me a silent chuckle as he begins shuffling through the papers on the table.

The mention of staying in Everton and Ryan has my mild filtering back to all those nights I spent alone with my thoughts while I was away. I told myself if I ever made it out of there, when I got out of the army for good, I'd come back for her. The only time I feel any peace is when I am wrapped in her arms.

I don't know if I can bring myself to walk away from her for a second time.

# Chapter Six

## RYAN

I'm busy setting up for my next appointment when the doorbell rings and the sound of Nadia's voice booms through the front lobby. Her cheery tone as she sings a good morning has the guys grumbling and a smile stretching across my face.

A few seconds later, I hear her knocking on the door as I turn to look at her short five-foot nothing frame.

"Hey," I say, pulling out the cleaning disinfectant to clean my station.

Nadia crosses the room, perching her hands on the edge of the counter before jumping up to take a seat. Her legs swing back and forth as she stares at me, waiting for me to say more. I know what she's doing here, what she's hoping to achieve, but I decide to make her beg a little.

"Cut to the chase. I want all the deets." She smiles, running her finger along her lower lip, waiting.

"What are you talking about?"

"Don't play coy with me. You know I hate that shit. Spit it the fuck out already," she finishes with a grin.

"I'm really not sure what you're talkin' about, but if you don't mind I have a client who should be here soon."

"Yeah, actually, I do mind. You might want to hurry and spit it out if you don't want to be late," she says, reclining back against the wall, folding her arms over her chest. "I'm not planning on going anywhere until you tell me what I want to hear."

Spinning around on my heel, I narrow my eyes at Nadia and toss my gloves down on the counter. The move earns me a loud giggle as I roll my eyes at her.

"There's really not much to tell. We hung out for a little bit and I gave him a ride home."

"Don't even try to lie to me, Ryan. You're terrible at it, you know that? I want to know the real deal. How many times did you two fuck? Did he go down on you? Was it everything you ever dreamed of and more?"

I hear Chris from the other side of the shop, his chair scraping across the floor as the music turns down. My head peeks over my shoulder as he holds the needle in one hand and his black gloved hand in the other. The look on his face says what I'm thinking, "what the hell is wrong with this girl?"

"It's nothing for you to be worried about," I say, raising my eyebrows before looking back at Nadia as I reach over to shut the door as Chris yells out a *fuck you*. Nadia flashes me an innocent smile, one that says she isn't the least bit sorry for involving one of my good friends in this conversation.

"Once and yes," I say, turning back around to finish setting up for my appointment.

"Yes, he went down on you or yes it was everything you've dreamed of?"

"Seriously?"

"As a heart attack. You promised, spill it."

"Yes, he went down on me."

I decide to ignore her other question, not wanting to get into how perfect the night had been. We were almost frantic in our reunion. It was as though we couldn't get enough of each other.

"You're a buzzkill. This isn't at all as exciting as I'd pictured it to be."

I smother my smile knowing how annoyed she is that I'm holding out on her.

"Alright, well, if you're not going to tell me what happened, will you at least tell me if you're planning on seeing him again?"

That was a question I had no problem answering.

"He said he's planning on staying in town for about a week and the plan is to spend time together while he's here."

As soon as the words pass my lips, the sound of the door ringing again has me opening the door to see who it is, wondering if it's my next appointment. I glance over at Nadia when I see my brother's large, stocky frame stalking toward us.

The moment her eyes fall on Dean's, as she turns back toward me, looking equally annoyed as she is sad. As much as she tries to act like she doesn't like Dean, I know it's the exact opposite.

She's always had the biggest crush on him, even back when we were in high school.

"Ryan," he says, resting his hands above the doorway before glancing over to where Nadia is sitting. A slow smile spreads across his face when he sees her sitting there, legs still swaying to the beat of the music playing overhead. This time though, she's looking down at her phone using it as a way to distract her from looking at him. It's a ploy to ignore him, to act like she's unaffected by his presence.

This girl has always had guys falling all over themselves to get her attention and when the one she wants does, she acts like he doesn't exist. Something happened with her and Dean back in the day, although she's never told me enough to fill in the blanks. With the way she just interrogated me about Maverick, I'd love to give her a dose of her own medicine, but there's something about the pain she's had on her face when she saw him tells me it would be a dangerous path to go down.

"What are you doing back in town?"

"I had to come back to get some things settled at Compass Security. I'll be heading back to Chicago on Monday," he says, pausing and looking back over at Nadia again. He's waiting for her to look up, to give him even a second of attention. He doesn't like how she's blowing him off, and I can't fault her for doing it.

His eyes look back over to me, his gaze adjusting from the way his eyes narrowed at Nadia back to me. He bites down on his lower lip, clearly lost in his thoughts before he continues.

"Listen, I have something I want to talk to you about before I head back out."

I put the rest of my stuff down, giving him my full attention.

"What's up?"

"Um, so I was just by the office and I ran into Maverick," he says, pausing as he gauges my reaction. He's trying to put his feelers out, to see how I'm going to react to the news.

Knowing where this is going, I cross my arms over my chest and give him my undivided attention. Nodding my head, I wave my hand out in front of me to urge him to continue.

"He was there with Graham. I should've told you about this before, but his dad passed away. I just wanted you to be aware he's in town, just in case you run into each other. Everton isn't all that big, so it's possible."

The sound of Nadia's sputtered laughter interrupts us, as my head jolts toward where she's sitting. Her phone is long since put away and her bright smile is stretched across her face, loving how my brother is seemingly clueless.

My eyes bug out at her, silently asking her to shut up. She'd love more than anything to point out to him how wrong he is about the whole situation.

Dean narrows his eyes before glancing back at me. I can see the questions swirling around in his head, wondering what the hell is going on.

"It's fine, Dean. You have nothing to worry about," I say, doing my best to reassure him despite my history with Maverick, there's nothing for him to be concerned over.

He remembers how hard it was for me after Mav left. Hell, I still remember how difficult it was for him to move past hearing the news his best friend had not only grown feelings and had a romantic relationship, if that's what you can even call it, with his sister, but after he got the news, the same best friend ended up running out of town.

Dean has admitted to me on more than one occasion he's sorry for the way he reacted and for any damage he may have done that led to Maverick leaving town. I know he's talked to Maverick about it after he left; he's told me about their conversations. Mav has reassured him his departure had nothing to do with their fight and everything to do with what went down with his dad.

"Listen, I know how much he means to you. As much as you both may try to act like you're not affected by him being in the same town. We've been talking to him about staying though, maybe helping Graham get things up and running at Compass Security here. It's inevitable you'll run into him. I also know he misses you. So, if you see him, at least give him a chance. Hear him out. Alright?"

As surprised as I am to hear him even acknowledge our feelings, I'm even more surprised to hear they offered him a job. As time went by, I never expected that he would come back, much less come back and stay, although I never gave up hope.

Having Dean acknowledge how much he meant to me tells me he wasn't oblivious to what was going on over all the years. Despite my best efforts, I have never been able to move on after he left.

Maverick has been the only person who's been in my heart all these years. He's the one

I've craved. I've yet to find anyone who makes my body ache the way he does.

"Alright," I say, not wanting to give him anymore. He may be able to read me, but I can tell he's not sure what to make of my short, clipped response.

His eyes narrow, waiting for me to say more, before I give him a small smile hoping to reassure him.

I hear him mutter how he has to get back to the office, but to call him later so we can meet up for dinner while he's still in town. I nod my head and manage to lift my hand to wave at him. My eye catches sight of the heart tattoo on my forearm and I bite my lip thinking about Maverick.

When he saw my ink, he couldn't keep his mouth off me. I replay the way his tongue danced across my skin. I never expected for something like that to be so erotic; it was almost mind-blowing.

Maverick promised me when he left he'd carry me with him, but I could tell, him finding out how I've carried him with me, both broke his heart but brought us together. It felt like we were joined in a way where, although it had been years since we had spoken or even seen each other, nothing had changed.

Things moved so fast between us after the first night he stayed with me, it was almost like that night joined us, cemented who we were to each other so that nothing could change it. No time, no distance, could erase the way I felt about him.

We were sent on a tailspin after Dean found out we had been seeing each other behind his back. If we hadn't been sneaking around, maybe Mav wouldn't have been trying to avoid going to the party without him. Maybe he wouldn't have taken his dad's truck which led to him getting in trouble and kicked out.

These are the same thoughts that have plagued me for years since he left. If anything would've happened differently, would he have stayed? Would we have gotten more time together? Would we be together now?

The sound of Nadia clearing her throat breaks through my thoughts as I glance over at her.

"You want to tell me what that was about?" I ask, probing her about the awkward tension that seems to envelop her when my brother steps into the room.

"You know how much I despise your brother, especially after what happened with you and Maverick."

"That's not the full story and you know it."

"I was there, and I do know. It may not have been the reason he got kicked out, but it's the reason he left town with nowhere to go, so he bailed. You and I both know it."

She's right, as much as I hate to admit it.

All of these questions are driving me nuts, only because I know she's trying to peel back a layer of a wound I've spent so much time trying to heal. She's trying to expose how I really feel about Maverick being back and I'm not sure I'm ready to go there just yet. I want to close my mind off to it and enjoy having him home. If I let myself feel the emotions I've worked to bury deep, I'll only be left heartbroken when he inevitably leaves.

Instead, I make the decision to soak up whatever time I have left with him, not wanting to let the idea of him staying change what is happening between us. All I've wanted was to see him again and now that he's back, I promise myself I'll enjoy it while it lasts.

I only hope my tattered heart can take it if he walks away again.

# Chapter Seven

## MAVERICK

The past few days have flown by. I spent most of yesterday at my dad's house. Going back to that place drudged up so many old memories I've kept at bay.

I told myself I only wanted to go get the shit he had kept of my mom's. Those were the only pieces of my life with him I would ever want to revisit. I found an old box in the bottom of his bedroom closet that kept a lot of her belongings. There were pictures in frames that once hung on the walls, her necklace with my birthstone, and even her wedding ring. Sitting in the front seat of my dad's truck, I arranged for the cleaning company to come in and clear out the house. Everything inside would be tossed out. They'd get it ready to be listed.

I wanted to wipe my hands of this whole place and never have to come back here.

Except that wasn't the truth. I did want to stay in Everton, simply because I wasn't prepared to say goodbye to Ryan.

All this time I've been avoiding trips back here, mostly not wanting to face all the terrible memories it would bring. As much as I hated my dad, I admit moving to Everton wasn't all bad. If my mom hadn't passed away, my dad would've never had been driven to leave. I would've never met Dean or Graham, which means I certainly never would've laid eyes on Ryan.

Ryan and I have spent time together every day since I've been back. My body still craves having her close, every bit as it once did. We haven't talked about what is still between us. I've never seen any sign she wanted it to stop, but Ryan was never one to openly confess her emotions. She keeps her hard exterior firmly in place like a defense mechanism.

The only time I've seen any sort of vulnerability shining through the cracked edges was when I pressed a kiss against the tattooed heart on her forearm. I recognized it immediately as being almost identical to the one she had drawn on her perfect skin all those years ago. Only now, the vines wrapped around it look more like barbwire, making it look like it's somehow keeping all the pieces of her heart together.

Opening the closet door, I pull out the bag where my newly pressed suit hangs. Laying it out on the bed, I head into the bathroom and turn on the shower so it's hot. The steam rises as I undress from my boxers and move to stand under the spray.

I stopped by the bar last night when Ryan was working. After a long day at my dad's house and a big day ahead at the funeral, I told her I was going to call it an early night. She was aware I had the funeral today and after I reassured her she didn't have to come, I decided to head out. It wasn't long after I came back to the hotel that I crashed.

Standing beneath the hot spray, my thoughts drift back to Ryan. My body aches for her, to have her close to me, especially after all this time. I stand under the water until the temperature turns cold. I'm not surprised that my lack of urgency in getting to the funeral home has me leaving twenty minutes later than I had planned.

Thankfully, I expect this will be a small gathering of only a few friends my dad had made in town and some family members that have traveled in to be here. My Aunt Patricia has made the trip to be here for me.

A few minutes before the services began, I see Dean and Graham enter through the doors.

"Thanks for being here," I say, reaching my hand out. Graham shakes it, using his other to clap me on the back as he says, "You know we wouldn't expect you to go through this on your own."

"That's right, man," Dean confirms, reaching around to give me a hug. I follow behind them as they take a seat, making my way toward the front of the room. Sitting with my hands in my lap, I listen as the minister talks about the life my dad has led and the heartbreak from the family he leaves behind.

I feel annoyed hearing him replay all the memories, from stories other family members have shared. I want to cut him off, tell him to stop talking when the sound of heels clicking on the tile floor provide a welcome distraction.

I look up to see Ryan standing next to me in a deep-red sweater and a pair of black, denim jeans. She's dressed in high-heeled boots, which completely take me off guard. Normally, you wouldn't find her in anything but a pair of DC's or Etnies.

Her makeup is dark; her blue eyes made captivating. The small smile that plays on her lips nearly knocks me backward. She rounds the side of the pew, side-stepping her way closer, before taking a seat next to me.

"Hey," I whisper to her, reaching over to wrap my fingers around hers.

She smiles up at me, a strand of her dark hair falling in front of her face. Keeping her hand wrapped in mine, I use my other arm to wrap around the back of the seat, pulling her to me.

It dawns on me for only a minute that Dean is here before the thought is immediately pushed out of my mind. Pressing a kiss against her hair, I turn toward the minister who continues to talk about all my dad has accomplished in his life. Yeah, he has had several achievements, most of which were before my mom passed.

Running my hand up and down her arm, I press my mouth against her ear and whisper,

"You really didn't have to come, but I can't lie, I'm so fuckin' glad you're here."

She tilts her head back to look at me. Her eyes bounce between my eyes down to my mouth and back up to meet my gaze. "Don't you think you should curb the swears, Mav? At least until we leave and are alone."

"I think you like my dirty mouth."

When her eyes trail back down to my mouth, I can't help but smile at the way she bites down on her lower lip. Seeing my reaction to her obvious perusal has her looking back up at me. I flash her a wink which earns me an eye roll as she turns to face forward again.

"I can think of about ten things I'd rather be doing right now with this mouth," I whisper against her hair.

A shiver rolls through her body as I run my hand back up her arm, knowing it has nothing to do with her body's temperature and everything to do with my whispered promises.

# Chapter Eight

## RYAN

After the funeral ended, Maverick disappeared to talk to the minister. Taking a seat outside on the bench, I wait for him. I'm not sure what he has planned for the rest of the evening, but knowing the primary reason for him coming back to Everton was for today, I want to make the most of whatever time I have left with him.

People filter in and out the front doors of the church. I turn my head when I hear Dean and Graham laughing as they jog down the front steps.

"I didn't expect to see you here today," Dean says, noticing me sitting here.

Glancing over at Graham, I see the look of apology on his face.

Looking back at Dean, he interrupts to say, "Hey, I'm going to take off. I wanted to swing by the office on my way home."

With a nod of his head, he mutters out a goodbye to Graham before turning his attention back on me.

"What do you want me to say? Yes, I've been seeing Maverick since he's been back. I don't really think it's any of your business though."

"Why didn't you tell me?"

"Once again, it's not any of your business."

His eyes narrow. His jaw set in place.

Yes, I know I'm being a bitch, but I really don't think he has a say in who I spend my time with. Yes, he is my brother and I want his support, but at the end of the day, I'm going to do what makes me happy.

"It's not like he's going to be here for long anyway."

Judging by the look on Dean's face, there is more he wants to say but I choose to let it go.

"I'm heading back to Chicago tomorrow afternoon. Maybe we can meet for lunch?"

"Yeah, sure."

"Alright, I'll text you tomorrow morning to make arrangements."

Dean reaches into the pocket of his dress pants and pulls out the key to his car. Hitting the fob button, his car starts in the mostly empty parking lot.

I watch as he jogs down the front steps toward where he's parked before he turns to face me.

"Oh, and, Ry, you can bring Maverick with you if you want. Despite what you may be telling yourself right now, I want you to be happy. If that means being with Maverick, I'll support whatever decision you make."

Without another word or a chance for me to respond, he turns around and continues down the stairs toward his BMW. I'm so lost in watching him pull out of his parking spot and drive out of the lot that I don't hear Maverick approach me.

"You didn't have to wait for me," he says as I gaze up at him, taking in the light dusting of facial hair lining his jaw.

"I was thinking we could stop and get dinner."

"I was actually thinking about heading back to the hotel and ordering in."

The disappointment creeps in and my heart aches over the rejection from him. I guess it's better this way. We don't need to spend every day together like we have been. It's only going to make saying goodbye more difficult.

"Alright," I say, taking a step closer to him and wrapping my arms around his waist. "I'll probably head home for the night then."

His arms slide around me as he leans in close, his nose against my shoulder.

"I don't want you to go."

I tilt my head back, trying to read his expression.

"You thought I meant I didn't want to hang out or have you come back to the room with me. That's not what I was trying to say."

I hate that he is reading me so well. I normally try so hard to keep my emotions in check, to not let anything affect me, yet having him around this week has brought all my walls down.

"No, I didn't," I lie, hating how vulnerable I feel. "I just figured you would want your space."

"Don't lie to me," he says, cutting me off.

I narrow my eyes at him. He's onto me though as his grin stretches across his face, slipping his arm around my neck, pulling me closer. He presses his mouth against my forehead, kissing me.

"Don't even try to say I don't know what I'm talking about. We both know I'm right and you'd rather be told to go streaking through the parking lot than admit you're wrong."

I roll my eyes dramatically.

"I mean, if you want to strip right here, you certainly won't see me complaining. It would delay our trip back to the hotel and what I have planned, but I'm all for getting started right here."

Smacking him on the chest, I take a step back and say, "Don't you wish."

"You're right, baby. I do fucking wish."

The entire way back to the hotel, I feel like I'm riding on a high. The adrenaline coursing through me makes it hard to keep my mind off what he has in store for the night. As soon as the elevator doors close, we can't keep our hands off each other. His strong hands wrap around my thighs, hoisting me up against the wall. His hard length rubs against me through the denim of my jeans and the move steals my breath away.

"You feel good, baby."

His warm breath feathers along my wet lips still tingling from his punishing kiss. I slip my hand around his neck, holding him closer to me.

The elevator dings, announcing our arrival, and the sound of a throat clearing clues us in that we are no longer alone.

"Excuse us," Maverick says, lowering me to the floor as he slides his hand in mine, tugging me along behind him out of the elevator.

I mutter an apology as we slip past the older couple. I can't help but chuckle at the grin on the gentleman's face when he gives me a wink.

Maverick quickly slides the key in the reader. The light flashes green and he quickly pushes the door open. He pulls me in behind him before slamming the door shut.

"God, you make me crazy. Now that I've had a taste of you, I'm like a starving man. Come here," he groans, pressing me up against the steel door as his mouth crashes down on mine.

I moan as my legs find their way home around his waist once again. He leans back, his eyes glossy and full of desire. He runs his hand over my chest, slipping beneath the cotton of my sweater. His callused fingers feeling rough against my soft skin.

"Mav," I choke out as his thumb rubs over my sensitive nipple.

With every tweak, he adds in a perfectly timed thrust against my aching center. Squeezing my eyes shut, I feel the arousal building, causing a shiver to roll through me.

Wrapping his hands around my thighs again, he keeps a hold of me as he carries me into the room, setting me on the edge of the bed.

Lifting my leg into the air, he slowly eases the zipper down on my boots. His eyes burn into mine as he slides them off my feet and tosses them onto the floor.  My breath hitches when his fingers curl into my denim jeans, pulling them, along with my underwear, down my legs. As soon as I'm bare beneath him, he drops to his knees with his mouth at my center. Sitting up, I peer down at him and watch as his mouth wraps around my aching clit, sucking.

"Holy shit," I mutter, dropping my head back between my shoulders.

His muffled moans add a vibration against my swollen bud as I lift my pelvis up, grinding against his face. His hands move to cup my ass, holding my body in the air as he buries his mouth between my legs.

"Yes, holy shit, yes. Don't fucking stop," I say, reaching down, holding him by his hair so he doesn't move. I fight against his tight grip to close my thighs around his head.

Lights flash before my eyes, and my body quivers with the force of my release. He doesn't relent, using his tongue to drive me so far out of my mind I can't form words or control my movements as I go speeding over the edge.

I feel my body twitch from the aftershocks of my release.

As my vision returns a moment later, I find Maverick standing at the foot of the bed with his pants down and his hard cock jutting out.

Cum leaks from the tip of his cock. My tongue skates across my lower lip at the thought of wrapping my mouth around him. My eyes trail up his body to find him dragging his thumb over his lip as he watches me spread out beneath him. His eyes are hooded, focused between my legs, as a smile plays on his lips.

His hand squeezes his length in a tight grip and I'm unable to resist any longer. As I slide down the bed before him, I take him by surprise when I wrap both of my hands around his shaft and guide his engorged head into my mouth, sucking as if my life depended on it.

His body moves on its own accord, pumping into my mouth as his hands clench into fists. I'm turned on again by how unrestrained he is, unable to control his movements. He may be using my mouth for his pleasure, but I know he's giving me the power I want now.

Keeping one hand rooted at the base of his cock, I wrap my other around his balls and trail my tongue down his shaft, taking one of his balls in my mouth.

"Mother fuckin' shit," he groans, widening his stance as he leans in closer, giving me better access to him.

"Mmm," I moan, trailing my tongue over to the other side and doing the same. His hands wrap in the strands of my long hair, holding me against him, but not controlling the movement. My hand fists his aching cock, pumping him up and down as I run my tongue over the sensitive flesh back up toward his tip before I suck him back into my mouth.

"Goddamn, Ryan," he groans, pumping into me over and over.

With my head tilted back and my tongue running beneath his hard length, he takes over sliding in and out of my mouth. Each stroke growing more and more urgent with his need to cum.

The look of pleasure mixed with pain on his face has my body taking over, wanting to see the pain fall away and replaced with the euphoria that he gave me a few minutes ago. With my lips wrapped tightly around him, he forces two hurried thrusts followed by a stream of swear words.

His eyes squeeze shut, tilting his head back. He lets out a deep grunt, rocking through me as I let out a moan, tasting his release.

He leans forward, pressing his mouth against mine. His tongue seeks mine, and I moan knowing his release is still on my tongue.

"You are a dirty little Rebel," he mumbles against my mouth. "I don't even want to know where you learned that. I don't want to picture you giving this to anyone but me, but fuck, it felt so good."

He pulls me to stand, pressing me against him as his hand slides down, gripping my bare ass. Squeezing the flesh in his hands, he slaps his hand down on my right cheek.

"Let's get you cleaned up," he mutters, wrapping his hands around my thighs.

I run my fingers through his short hair, focusing on nothing but the feel of him pressed against me as he carries me to the bathroom.

I've wanted this man for as long as I can remember, and the thought of him leaving again makes my heart ache.

# Chapter Nine

## MAVERICK

I reach my hand beneath the faucet, checking the temperature before I lean over and plug the drain. Standing, I feel the breath of air sucked out of my lungs when my eyes fall on Ryan. She looks beautiful with her long, brown hair falling over her shoulder. My eyes drag over her body as she peels the material of her shirt over her head and unhooks her bra, letting it fall to the floor.

In one swift movement, I grab the hem of my shirt and quickly pull it over my head. I let my gaze fall over her smooth, tan skin, over the ink that wraps around her arm and down her leg. The ink looks so much like the drawn-on designs she once wore.

Thinking of her back then has memories of our first night together flashing through my mind. Remembering how beautiful she looked beneath me, tasting her lips and every inch of her skin as I catalogued what I thought would be our last night together.

I would've thought coming back to Everton after all these years would've been harder. Having to face my dad and everything I left behind is difficult, but having Ryan at my side has only solidified who she was through some of my most difficult times.

Even before I acted on my feelings for her, her mere presence always had the ability to ease the pain I carried with me. Her fire and passion shined a light in the bleak darkness.

Drawing myself out of my thoughts, my eyes focus on Ryan's face. Her eyebrows are furrowed as her eyes try to decipher what I am thinking.

Turning, I lean forward and pull her into a deep kiss. She reaches up onto her tiptoes, meeting me halfway, as her arms wrap around my neck, pulling me close.

"Let's get in before the water turns cold," I whisper against her lips.

She nods her head and moves to step into the bathtub.

Reclining against the side of the tub, I open my legs as she slides in between them, resting her back against my chest.

"It's been so nice being with you this week. Thank you for coming today. I know I said you didn't have to, but it meant a lot to have you there."

She tilts her head back, resting it on my shoulder as her eyes gaze up at mine.

"You don't have to thank me. I wanted to be there for you."

Her fingers wrap around mine as she continues, "I know it wasn't easy for you to come back to Everton. I know it may not seem like it, but I've always been here, for whatever you need."

For as long as I can remember, I've dealt with everything on my own. The things I've witnessed during my time in the military is not the type of shit you want to burden other people with. It's enough to make it difficult for anyone to rest easy when they lie down at night.

"Have you thought about what you're going to do now the funeral is over?"

I sense a hint of hesitation in her voice as she turns to focus her attention ahead.

"I got a message from the realtor this morning on my way to the church that someone put in an offer on the house. I'd already told him the first offer we receive we're going to accept. I want to wipe my hands of this place."

I'm not sure if it's the bitterness in my tone or what I said, but I feel Ryan's body tense against mine as she moves to turn and face me. It's distracting really, having Ryan's naked body on display for me, but the look on her face clues me in that she's not at all interested in the two of us being naked in here together.

"So, I guess this is it then? You're not going to take Graham and Dean up on the offer to work at Compass?"

My eyes narrow. "I thought you knew I wasn't planning on staying here long. I have to report back to base next week."

She nods her head, biting her lip. Her eyes focus somewhere else, lost in her own thoughts.

"Can you tell me one thing? What was this to you then? You come back here and drudge up all these old feelings. What was the point, Maverick?"

"Are you kidding me? It's not like that and you know it. I care about you more than anyone, so don't demean what this is."

Her jaw clenches, shaking her head as her eyes look away. "Are you planning on coming back or is this it?"

"Ryan, I have a duty to my country and to the men who are still over there serving. I would never ask you to walk away from your art; I know how much that means to you."

"You wouldn't have to ask, Maverick."

She shoots up, the water cascading down her body as she grabs for the towel and wraps it around her naked body.

I want to stop her, to pull her back against me and hold her but I don't.

"What's that supposed to mean?"

"If it came down to it, choosing between this life and you, I'd choose you. That's where we're different. I've spent the past four years hoping and waiting for you. I told you I wasn't going to give up. I thought this was it. I thought you were finally coming back but I was wrong."

"It was only a matter of time though, right? You left me once, I should've known it was bound to happen again. I'm just glad this time I was worth more than waking up to you gone with only a letter left behind. For as long as I've known you, you've kept yourself locked up and closed off. I didn't push you. I didn't want to because I thought if you got to see how much I cared, eventually you would trust me enough to let me in fully but you never gave me a chance. I know what happened with your dad back then had to have been tough, but you didn't have to give up. You didn't have to walk away. As much as I want to spend however much time I have left with you, I can't do this to myself again."

"Ryan, wait..." I shout as she turns, opens the door and walks out.

"God dammit," I mumble as I stand up and grab a towel. I quickly dry off, wrapping a towel around my waist, hoping to stop her before she leaves.

"Will you just hang on? Stop and talk to me." I hold my hand out, wanting to pull her against me. My heart is beating wildly, like a caged animal in my chest.

I watch as she swiftly pulls her jeans up her legs, sliding them beneath the towel that still wraps around her chest. I hate that even now, she's covering herself up from me. How did things go so terribly wrong in just a matter of a few minutes? I didn't want it to be like this.

"What more is there left to say?"

"Ryan, I can't give you what you want. That's not who I am, as much as I want it to be."

Ryan scoffs, shaking her head as she picks up her bra and turns away from me to finish dressing.

"Will you just look at me?"

"Maverick, I honestly can't bear the thought of looking at you right now. I still replay the last night we had together through my head and I don't want to memorize the look on your face as you tell me goodbye."

I hate the sound of her voice right now. I sense the wall she had let down around me go up, blocking me out. The worst part is I know there is nothing I can do or say to her right now that's going to help her feel better.

When she's finished dressing, I watch her as she walks around the room and grabs the boots she was wearing. Sitting on the edge of the bed, she slides her feet in and zips them up her calves.

"Please just stay," I mutter. The words sound distorted even to myself.

Glancing up at me, her eyes stare into mine. I know now what she meant when she said she didn't want to remember the look on my face because seeing the heartbreak behind her eyes tears my heart in two.

"I'm not going to stay to appease your own guilt, Maverick. I know you feel this between us and it's bullshit that you're going to take the easy way out and leave. I just want you to remember when you go that it wasn't me who left. I'm not walking away from you because it's what I want. I'm walking away because I don't have a choice. You are not and never will be mine; I realize that now. I hope you take care of yourself."

Reaching down, she grabs the strap to her purse and slides it over her head. The sound of my phone ringing echoes through the quietness of the room, mixing with the loud beating of my heart drumming in my ears.

Crossing the room, I pick up my phone from where I tossed it on the nightstand and check the caller ID. The number is listed as unknown.

"I'm sorry, I have to take this."

"Of course," she says as I hold the phone to my ear and answer.

As soon as the call connects and I hear Sergeant Jackson's voice filter through the phone, I know whatever it is will change everything. Whatever I thought it was going to be, nothing had prepared me for the news I was about to receive.

My eyes close as the dam breaks, unleashing tears unlike anything I've felt since losing my mom. I'm reminded that nothing in this life is guaranteed and anything can change in a moment's notice.

His words sound distorted as he relays the details of the mission gone wrong. My heart aches for my friends who lost their lives and for the ones who are fighting to hang on in a hospital in Germany.

Fighting through the tears, I glance around the room hoping to find Ryan still here with me only to find that I'm all alone.

It hits me hard that I just let go of the only good thing I've had in my life. It's that realization that allows the darkness to emerge and threatens to swallow me whole.

# Chapter Ten

## RYAN

Swinging open the front door of Tattered, I hear *Evenge Sevenfold* blaring through the speakers. Chris glances up from his workstation before turning his attention back to what he's working on.

Andi is seated in the office chair, reclined back with her feet up on the desk with a magazine in her hand. Distracted by the music, she doesn't seem to pay attention to me or maybe she's so out of it she doesn't even hear the doorbell.

"Excuse me!" I shout over the music. That must be the wakeup call she needs as it forces her into action, setting her feet on the floor and pressing her hand against her chest.

"Holy hell!" she shouts back before holding the remote up to the stereo, bringing the volume down to a more manageable level.

"You going to get up and actually do some work around here?"

"I'm sorry, I was taking a break."

The foot traffic in and out of the shop is very rarely slow. We are one of the leading tattoo shops in the area, which is saying a lot considering the size of Des Moines. Growing up in Everton, it was nice having a small town feel not too far away from the big city. It made it an easy decision when we were deciding where to open our shop, knowing having it here would be the best place to bring in new customers.

"Break is up. I can think of a hundred things that you could be doing that are not putting your feet up on my fucking desk. If you want a break, go get a coffee, then come back and get to it."

I add that on the end to make it less angry because despite how annoyed I was coming in to see her like that, I'm actually in a good mood.

I spend the next twenty minutes going through my schedule for the upcoming week.

Maverick will be leaving soon and the best way for me to keep my mind off him leaving is by keeping occupied.

I haven't spoken to Maverick in a week since our fight. After I stormed out of the hotel room, I swore to myself I wasn't going to put myself through the heartbreak of reaching out to him. He was the one who was in the wrong here, not me.

Truth be told, I had every expectation of never hearing from him again. That didn't stop me from driving by the hotel every morning on my way to get coffee. It was pointless really; I could've walked to the coffee shop. I knew what I was doing though.

I wanted to see if he had left town yet. I've spent every minute since I left preparing myself for it to happen. It wouldn't be the first time he walked away without giving me much of an explanation.

The weight I felt lift off my chest when I saw his dad's pickup parked in the hotel parking lot felt like a ten-ton boulder being released from my chest. He hasn't been driving it; I'm not sure if it's because it was his dad's and the resentment he holds toward him, or if being in the pickup brings back memories of us.

I know he was dead set on selling it before he left town and I didn't think he'd leave without doing so just because we got into an argument. I even called the hotel to see if he had checked out and they confirmed he still had reservations. I could've easily found out his plans if I called Dean and asked, but I was forcing myself to move on from Maverick. Or at least that's what I was telling myself I've been doing.

After picking up my coffee, I went back to my place and grabbed my notebook. I was going to sit at my desk and do some sketching. It was something I often did when I had a lot on my mind. Feeling more awake, I snagged my board from where it sat against the wall. Sticking my notebook and pencils into my backpack, I take off with no real destination in mind.

I needed some fresh air and I knew wherever I ended up would leave me inspired.

The feeling of the warm breeze against my face and the sunlight beating down heated my skin. I was dressed in a black tank top and a pair of skinny jeans, topped off with my signature snapback. My sun-kissed skin still looked bronze from my trip out to California and I promised myself to try and keep the warm glow through the rest of the summer.

The sound of the wheels beat against the cracks on the concrete, using my right foot to help pick up speed. I wasn't planning on coming down here when I left, but the closer I got to the water, the slower I went.

I've continued to come down by the river, the place where Maverick and I spent my birthday together, over the years.  Although, now that I think about it, it's been a few months since I've been down here. It was just after the cooler weather started to warm up and I found myself anxious to claim my board again.

Using my foot to press down on the back of the worn wood, I skid to a stop in front of the dock. There is a park down by the Cedar River with picnic tables and trails, winding around the edge of the water. Setting my board on the grass underneath an old oak tree, I lean against the tree and slide my bag between my feet.

Reaching inside, I pull out my notebook and start flipping through the pages of drawings I've kept over the years. I never got rid of the notebook Maverick gave me. I only pulled it out when I found that the memories got to me too much.

Stopping on one of the pages, I let my finger trace over the word 'rebel' etched on the page.

Flipping to the next, I look at the heart I had drawn as a sketch of the tattoo that now lives on my skin. The heart looked a lot like the one Maverick had asked about on our first night alone together. Only now, the heart in this picture looks every bit of the one I felt beating in my chest after he left.

Looking back now, I was so young and naïve to think that I could so blindly open myself up to him and share parts of me I hadn't even told my best friend. He may have been Dean's best friend, but Maverick was still a stranger to me on the outside. I had given my heart to a stranger and even after all these years, I feel like I still haven't got it back.

I was so willing to give myself to him that I left myself unprotected. In doing so, he took my heart and left it torn and tattered, barely beating. I remember when I drew this tattoo, I promised myself I wouldn't be so reckless with it again. I would guard myself and remember what it felt like to barely get by every day.

My fingers run along his initials, which I hid in the shading of the tattoo. When Chris transferred the sketch to ink, I asked him to make sure that he kept them there. Looking at a glance, you'd likely never even notice them, but

I knew they were there and that was all that mattered to me.

I had let my mind drift off, remembering all those emotions I felt when I was drawing, that I never even heard the pickup pull up in the parking area not too far from where I was sitting. I certainly never heard Maverick get out of the truck and walk up to me, peering over me as the memories crash over me in waves.

"You okay?" The sound of his voice coming out is more of a grumble taking me off guard.

Flipping the notebook shut, I hold it against my chest and peek up at him. The sunlight behind him makes it difficult to see. He steps closer, using his body to shield the light from my eyes.

"Yeah. What are you doing here?"

"I was driving down to meet up with Graham and saw you on your skateboard," he stops, looking out onto the water as if he's lost in thought before his eyes drag back down to mine. "When I saw you stop here, I waited, not sure if I should approach you. But then you took out your notebook and I couldn't help myself. Can I see?"

His hand reaches out, pointing to the notebook now pressed against my chest. My heart rate picks up and my palms turn sweaty as I glance down, not sure what to say or how to respond.

I think he senses my hesitation, dropping his hand to his side. My eyes dart to his. His jaw is set, making his expression unreadable.

"I'm not sure you deserve the right anymore," I croak.

My words hit him like a punch to the gut. Running his palm over his jaw, his eyes focus on the ground.

"I guess you're right," he says, looking up at me.

I almost regret my words when I see the hurt on his face.

"Listen, about the other night, I know I shouldn't have said what I said. I've been doing a lot of thinking—"

Holding my hand up, I stop him. "Maverick, I don't think we owe each other an explanation anymore. I mean, you said it, you had no intentions of moving back to Everton. Your focus is on your job, I get that, because right now that's where mine is, too. Let's just leave this at what it is, a really great week with two friends who were catching up."

His nostrils flare at the mention of us being friends and I can't help but feel the same. Calling what is between us friendship is bullshit. There isn't a bone in my body that wants to be friends with Maverick, but I know that I love and care about him enough that if that's the only capacity I can have him, I'm willing to accept him.

The growl that emanates from deep within his chest has my head jolting up toward him as he falls to his knees down in front of me.

"You didn't let me finish and I'll be damned if you think that's what I want. I may not have had intentions of moving back to Everton, but it doesn't mean I never planned to come back for you."

Reaching his hands out, he runs them down my forearms toward mine.  Letting the notebook fall back into my lap, I look up at him. He's struggling with what he's about to say but I don't stop him.

"After you left, I got a call." He stops, squeezing his eyes shut as he lets out a stuttered breath. He's on the verge of tears and this is a side of Maverick I've never seen.

"When I found out my dad died, I left my platoon early. My sergeant told me they were only expecting it to be a few more days before they would be coming home. Otherwise, I would've had my dad's funeral sooner and left to head back out with them. Anyway, the call I got was from my sergeant. I guess some of the guys were on surveillance duty when the Humvee they were riding in hit a roadside bomb. Two of them didn't make it and the other two are in critical care. I don't know—" he pauses, squeezing his eyes shut again not wanting to voice the words out loud.

Setting my notebook down, I move to climb onto his lap and I'm grateful he lets me. Wrapping my arms around him, I press my lips against his neck and send up a silent prayer of thanks. I know the reality of the situation because I've spent many nights lying awake at night thinking about getting the same news. The one saying something happened to him and he wouldn't be making it home, at least not alive.

I feel Maverick's body shake as the sobs rack through his body and my heart breaks for him. He's felt so much loss in his life, it's no wonder he struggles to let anyone close to him.

His arms wrap around my lower back, rubbing his fingers along the skin beneath my tank top. There is so much I want to say to him in that moment. I want him to know that I'm here for him, that I'm not going anywhere. There is another part of me that realizes that his dad dying saved his life, because he would've been there and the way he's feeling now, could've been me.

"I need you to know I'm sorry," he mutters, his words coming out broken.

"We don't have to talk about that—" I say.

"No. We do," he interrupts, stopping me as my eyes meet his. "I have been thinking this week, especially about my friends' wives who are grieving the loss of their husbands. I want you to know I made a mistake. I shouldn't have let you go. I know how you felt when I left you because watching you go, I couldn't do it. All of this has just reminded me that I can't take us for granted. I love you; I've been in love with you since I was thirteen years old and you flew past me on your skateboard nearly knocking me on my ass. I don't care where I go or what I do because being with you is what will make me happy. I can live anywhere in this world because as long as I'm with you, I'm home."

Tears fill my eyes. I bite down on my lower lip, struggling to keep my emotions in check. I've spent so many nights lying awake missing him.

My heart and body have ached to have him with me, to hear those words pass his lips.

"It's not my fault. You were the one who got in my way. You were following me around, even then."

A grin breaks out across his face. I can't help it. My heart warms as a curve lines my mouth, matching his.

Wrapping my hand around his neck, I run my thumb along the edge of his jaw. "I love you, too. I promise there is no one who will ever love you like I do."

"Well, that's good, because I don't want anyone but you."

I scoff, laughing. "You better fucking not," I murmur as my lips crash down on his. His arms wrap around me tight, holding me close to him.

# Epilogue

## MAVERICK
### One Month Later

My knuckles rasp on Graham's office door. He glances up from the papers he was shuffling through, looking at me. His hair looks like he's ran his hands through it and his facial hair is longer than he normally keeps it.

I don't dare mention it though. He's been on edge lately and if I had to guess, it has everything to do with the five-foot-four blonde who has kept him on his toes since we were in high school.

"I'm going to head out for the night. Ryan and I are having a date night tonight."

It's been three weeks since I returned home from attending the funerals. Originally Ryan wasn't going to be able to come with me. I flew out to Georgia and much to my surprise, she showed up at my hotel room the next morning. I was so fucking grateful to have her there with me. Going through this without her would've been hard, especially because I've been feeling guilty for not being there.

I've been struggling with nightmares, survivor's guilt as my therapist calls it. I keep feeling like had I been there, maybe the situation would've turned out differently. Sleeping next to Ryan has always brought me a sense of peace, but when the nightmares started in, she insisted that I talk to someone. I know she was worried and I hated that, so I did what she asked.

As hard as it's been for me to open up and talk to people, I'm glad she's pushed me to do this. Now I'm taking doc's advice and taking my girl out for the night. Ryan and I skipped past the dating stage. Time has never really been in our favor, so we decided to take a few steps back and enjoy taking things slow. Which is really kind of silly if you ask me because after I told her how I felt for her, I insisted that I wasn't going to leave her again. That also meant that for as long as we're together, I won't go to bed another night without her by my side.

We've been talking a lot about moving out of her loft and finding a place with a little more space, but for now, we're just enjoying each other.

"Alright, sounds good. Have a good night, man. I'll see you next week."

When I decided to stick around Everton, I knew without a doubt I wanted to help Dean and Graham get their business off the ground. It was also great to work with my friends, especially after everything that has happened.

A few minutes later, I pull up in front of Tattered and park next to Ryan's Jeep. Pushing the button on my remote, I lock up and decide to head inside the shop knowing she's likely still finishing up.

The bell rings as I walk through the front door and I spot Ryan in her room off to the side. I nod my head at Chris, giving him a silent hello before heading over to see my girl.

She's cleaning up for the day. Leaning against the doorway, I watch her cross the room and bend down to put something away.

"Damn," I mutter to myself. I didn't think she'd hear me over the music, but I must've been talking louder than I expected.

"You like what you see?" she replies over her shoulder, not even bothering to look over at me.

"You know I do." Moving on impulse, I cross the room and wrap my hands around her waist, pulling her up. She turns to face me, sliding her hands over my chest.

Leaning down, I press a kiss against her lips. Her hand is touching a place on my chest that's still sore from the tattoo she recently designed, now permanently displayed on my skin.

"How's it feeling?"

"Not bad, I think it's healing pretty well."

Her hands wrap around the hem of my shirt, pulling it up so she can take a look. The tattered heart resembles the one that she has on her forearm, but the talent she put into the design symbolizes so much more than that for me. The flag that wraps around the heart, like a shield of protection. It's perfect and I'm proud to have her heart with me now, wherever I go.

She leans forward and presses a soft kiss against my skin and I feel the jolt shoot through me. Ryan's always had this effect on me.

Wrapping my hand in her hair, I tilt her head up and press another kiss against her lips. Only this time, I deepen it as my tongue tangles with hers.

"Baby, you should be careful. We have plans for tonight but with the look in your eyes, I think I'd much rather take you upstairs and stay in for the night."

"Our reservations aren't for another hour. I'm sure we could make use of our time until then, don't you think?"

The desire on her face and the swollen look of her lips gives me ideas of my own. Ones that have nothing to do with making it for our dinner plans.

"You're fucking perfect for me, you know that?"

"Wasn't it just this morning you were calling me a pain in your ass?" she asks, raising her eyebrow as her lips curve into a small smile.

She knows how to drive me crazy and right now she's doing it again.

Reaching down, I wrap my hand around her ass cheek and squeeze her flesh through the tight denim of her jeans.

"I'm glad you reminded me. You still owe me for that little tease this morning. I guess we'll have to make use of that hour before dinner after all."

I press her body against the counter, rubbing my hard length against her. She hitches her leg over my hip as a deep moan passes her lips.

"Fucking perfect," I mutter as my mouth crashes down on hers.

This girl has ruined me.

Thank you for reading the Tattered Heart Duet! I hope you love Maverick and Ryan as much as I do.

I appreciate your help in spreading the word, including telling a friend. Reviews help readers find books! Please leave a review on your favorite site.

If you loved Torn and Tattered, I'd love to give you a sneak peek at my A Heart's Compass series. Do you remember Graham, Maverick's friend? He has his own story titled Until I Found You! It's a small town, second chance romance. You can start the series with Where I Found

You or jump into Until I Found You and read Graham's story today!

You can sign up for my newsletter to learn more about my new releases. You can also join my Facebook group, Brooke O'Brien's Rebel Reader Group, for exclusive giveaways and sneak peeks of future books. To join, visit:

www.authorbrookeobrien.com/follow.

Now, turn the page for a sneak peek of Until I Found You…

# Until I Found You

A HEART'S COMPASS
BOOK THREE

USA TODAY BESTSELLING AUTHOR
## BROOKE O'BRIEN

# Chapter One

## HALLE

"Woah, we're half-way there," I sing, as I furious-ly massage the conditioner into my hair. "Woah, livin' on a prayer."

I'm not quite sure why I'm singing this song, but it's fitting for this morning. I'm the type of person who sings when I'm trying to focus or when I'm in a hurry. Although I can't sing when I'm trying to read a street sign. I'm one of those people who turns down the radio to see what's fifteen feet in front of me. That's neither here nor there right now.

The point is, I'm running late, and I need all the help I can get. It would come to the surprise of no one that I'm running behind schedule. In fact, if there's one thing you could ever count on, it's that I'm usually two or ten steps behind everyone else.

I get distracted easily, get caught up staring off at whatever shiny object has stolen my attention, like right now. Which is why I'm singing to myself as I stand in the shower, rushing through the process of washing my hair.

I have twenty minutes in which to make it to the Hopeful's Bridal Boutique on the other side of our small town of Arbor Creek. Today is a big day for Ellie, one of my best friends, as she'll hopefully find the dress she's been searching for.

In all honesty, it's not Ellie I'm worried about who will be ticked at me for arriving fifteen minutes past the time I was supposed to be there. No, not at all. It's my roommate and other best friend, Kinsley. She's the yin to my yang. It's what makes our friendship balance out—everything I'm not, she makes up for by pushing me to be.

Kinsley would never be caught dead arriving late for anything. It's more likely she would arrive fifteen to twenty minutes early, with a checklist of everything she needs to do. I'm more of a fly-by-the-seat-of-my-pants kind of girl. I don't have much of my life planned out. I don't even know what I'm going to wear today, let alone have I thought ahead on where I see myself in five years.

I keep Kinsley young and she reminds me to never take life too seriously because, let's face it, we're all going to end up at the same place. I can't take any of this shit with me anyway. I just hope I arrive late when I go too.

Leaning my head back, I let the suds wash away before I run my hand over my long hair, wringing out the water before reaching down to turn off the faucet.

Reaching outside the shower, I blindly pat around for the towel I set on the rack. Grabbing it, I pull it toward me and use it to pat dry my face as the sound of hard knocking pounds against the door.

"Shit. Shit," I groan to myself, realizing I had spent far too much time in the shower. Along with Ellie and Kinsley, our good friend, Brea, who rounds out our little biker gang of badassery is joining us for today. Brea's dating the brother of Ellie's fiancé, so really, she's her sister-in-law for all intents and purposes.

There's a pounding at the door that comes for a second time, spurring me into action. Brea was supposed to be here any minute now, so we could ride together.

Wrapping the towel around my body, I tiptoe my way out of the bathroom and down the hallway. I can imagine the look Kinsley would have on her face if she were to witness this moment, knowing I'm leaving drops of water on the hardwood floor behind me.

This is why we're friends. She needs to learn not to sweat the little things, like water on your floor. It will dry on its own.

Clutching the towel to my chest, I don't bother even looking out the window as I swing the door open and turn back around.

"Hey Brea," I call out over my shoulder, "give me just a second to get dressed, and we'll head out."

Moving quickly, I'm mindful to step around my little puddles of water, careful not to slip and fall, as I head back down the hall toward my bedroom when the sound of his deep voice hits me.

We're usually not prepared for the moments that change our lives. I didn't see it coming the day Graham Shaw broke my heart, shattering it into a million pieces. I thought he was going to be in my life forever, but it turns out forever came sooner than I had expected.

Which brings me to this moment. For a second, I question if this is a cruel version of déjà vu, only now I don't want to believe my ears. Jolting myself into place, I squeeze my eyes shut hoping that what I just heard was all in my head and not at all what I thought it was.

"Do you always open the door to strangers and invite them in, without even checking to see who it is?"

Turning slowly, I wish I would've prepared myself better for what, or rather whom, I was about to see.

My eyes narrow and it takes me a second to collect myself, getting over the shock of seeing Graham Shaw standing before me in all his handsome glory.

"I didn't realize you were a stranger," I bite back, realizing the way he had left me with so many unanswered questions still hits like a hard slap to the face, even after all this time.

My eyes stare intently, as I hold the towel wrapped around me tight. It feels like all the air has been sucked out of the room and of me, reflecting on how much weight is carried in one sentence alone.

If I didn't know any better, I'd say there was a look of guilt that passes over his face, but before I can analyze it further, it's gone. His jaw flexes, as his eyebrows furrow, looking back at me.

I never had expected to be a stranger to Graham, yet now it seems like that's who we are.

It's a weird feeling staring back at the man you loved more than anything. Remembering all the things you knew about him, like the way he used to bite his lip when he was deep in thought or how he'd crack his knuckles when he was nervous.

Looking at the man in front of me, I can't help but feel as though I don't know anything about him. It was hard to get through every day after he left. It almost feels like a lifetime since I last saw him.

Damn, he looks good though. I used to love running my hand over his pecs down to his abs. He always worked out, but when he was younger, he was lean despite years of football and lifting weights. He's filled out more and it pains me to say it, but time was so good to him.

It makes me even more angry to think about all the women he's attracted since then.

"I know you better than you know yourself, Halle. Don't be fooled. I don't understand why the hell you'd open the door and let someone in, not realizing who's on the other side. It's not safe. I could've been anyone."

"First of all, it's been five years. You knew who I was then, but I'm not that girl anymore, Graham. You don't know me at all. Second, if you weren't paying attention when I answered the door, I thought you were my friend, Brea. I didn't think you were just anyone."

His eyebrows raise higher and I realize then if he hadn't felt guilty before, he does now. Maybe even a little shocked too.

"You always were a pain in my ass," he mutters to himself, running a hand over his face and down over his jaw.

In doing so, I watch as he stares back at me and for the first time since walking into my apartment, he lets his eyes roam over my face to my neck and down over the rest of my body. When he finds his way back up, I meet his stare with my eyes narrowed into slits. His stare is so blatant, his eyes burning into every inch of me.

"You used to love that about me," I retort.

A small smile curves at his lips. The mention of the past and what we used to be stings, like a zap to the heart. I had closed all roads to my heart where Graham was concerned a long time ago.

I'm not going down this same road with him again. Not anymore. He had his chance.

"Well, listen, this little reunion has been fun and all, but I have to get going. My friend is gonna be here any minute. So, if you don't mind telling me what the hell you're doing here, that'd be great. That way I can send you back on your way."

The curve of Graham's smile grows, and I want to roll my eyes and demand him to leave.

"Mm, there's the fire," he smirks.

I kid you not, the fucker has the gall to smirk at me. He always loved getting me riled up. I want to smack him upside the head, he makes me so angry.

"Tick, tock. I don't have all day."

"Are you talking back to me right now, Halle?"

"Yes, Graham, that's how conversations with me work. Now get to the point."

Chuckling, he crosses his arms, which leaves me momentarily distracted as my eyes roam over him, taking in the way his muscles bulge when he flexes.

"Kinsley sent me here. Something about helping her roommate load up some things for her for Callum and Ellie's wedding. Do you know anything about that?"

"Kinsley." I pause, feeling the edge of irritation seep into my tone. "I'm sorry, you said Kinsley sent you over here?"

Of course, she did. If there's anyone in my life who hoped Graham and I would end up together, it was Kinsley. In fact, she had our whole wedding planned out for us, knowing exactly every detail we'd want for our big day.

She really missed her calling as an event planner because I swear, the woman is as organized as she is frustrating right now.

"Yeah, I was down at the salon a little bit ago. She helped get me in for a haircut under short notice, so I was doing her this favor in return."

I want to ask him what he's even doing here. Why he's in Arbor Creek when he made it clear when he left that he was never going to return, at least not this soon. As much as it's killing me to ask, I leave it alone.

It's a dead end road and, quite frankly, I don't have it in me to care anymore.

"That's funny, considering Kinsley helped me load everything up last night," I deadpan, looking at Graham unamused.

"Is that right?" He laughs, just as my phone pings with a text message.

Turning on my heel, I continue down the hallway toward my bedroom to grab my phone.

**Brea: I'm stuck in traffic on the highway. I'm sorry, I'll have to meet you there.**

*Ugh!* Locking my phone, I toss it absentmindedly somewhere on my bed. Opening my drawer to my dresser, I grab my black lace bra and matching panties. Dropping my towel, I make quick work of putting them on while sauntering across my room toward my closet to figure out what to wear.

Looking in the corner mirror, I see Graham eyeing me from where he still stands rooted in place in our entryway. There's a fire in his gaze, one that's been a long time since I've seen, but remember from all those years ago.

I let him drink me in standing before him, reminding him of everything he let go of when he chose to run away rather than face his problems head on.

It's terrible of me to say, knowing the series of events which led him to leaving, but it doesn't change the fact he hurt me when he did.

Seeing him look at me the same way he did all those years ago lights something within me that's been burned out, withering away for a long time. I've tried to move on, used meaning-less relationships with nameless guys as a way of burying my feelings for him.

Staring back at him, I wonder if he's having the same thoughts I am, about how time and distance has changed things between us but the connection between us is still there.

I feel confident and sexy, watching the way his eyes eat up every inch of my body, down to my painted red toes back up over my chest and to my face.

"If that's all, don't let the door hit you on the way out, Graham. Travel safe when you head back to Chicago," I say, opening the closet to search for something to wear.

Peeking my head out from behind the door, I spot Graham reaching down to adjust himself. Biting my lip, I clear my throat as his eyes dart over meeting mine.

"Oh, and do me a favor, will ya?" I smile, loving how wound up he looks, waiting for what I'm about to say.

My smile widens, knowing I have him right where I want him. "Lock the door for me when you go. I wouldn't want anymore strangers showing up at my door and inviting themselves inside."

Leaving him with a wink, I force myself to focus on what I'm doing. I'm glad he can't see me now because my cover would be blown.

I'm so spaced out, thinking about the way he looked at me, that I can't even think straight.

My ears perk, listening for any signs of him leaving. I hear him mutter something about me being a pain in his ass followed by shuffling feet before the door opens. The sounds from outside filter into the apartment and down the hall, then a moment later the door closes once again.

Stepping out from behind the closet door, I take a seat on the edge of the bed and fall back, looking up at the ceiling fan spinning around.

Graham is the only man who's ever made my heart beat out of my chest.

What he's doing back in Arbor Creek, I have no idea, but I'm glad to see him again.

# Chapter Two

## HALLE

Leaning over into the trunk of my car, I carefully stack the third box onto the pile before slowly lifting them into my hands. Feeling shaky, I pause and let out a slow breath. I probably should save myself the stress of carrying three boxes of breakables inside, but my momma didn't raise no bitch. Why make two trips when I can get this done in one?

Slowly and carefully, I make my way toward the front of the Hopeful's carrying the boxes of wine glasses and the vases that I ordered on Amazon. The clock is starting to wind down, we're just a couple months away from when Callum and Ellie walk down the aisle.

Taking the step on the curb, I peer into the front of the boutique window and see my girlfriends huddled in a circle. My eyes widen, flashing them with a hard look that says, "one of you pay attention to me and help me open the damn door." As if picking up on my laser focus, Kinsley turns and sees me. Her eyes widen, taking in the stack of boxes in my arms before rushing toward the door to help usher me in.

"What the heck are you doing? You could drop those! And what took you so long to get here?" she mutters, holding the door open for me.

"What are you talking about?" I ask, playing coy. I know she's aware of the fact I'm late. Twenty minutes according to the clock in my car, but I'm playing it off like I'm early. I like to give her hell, it's one of my favorite things to do. Considering she's the reason why Graham showed up at my door this morning, I feel like she deserves it. I'm still not sure if I should be annoyed or mad at her for it yet.

It's why she's my soul mate. She helps balance me out, keep me in line. Most days I love her for it, but days like today when I'm stressed to the max and feeling the error of my ways, I don't want to hear her obvious disapproval.

"We were supposed to be here at nine thirty. It's nine fifty-two, Halle. What took you so long?"

Setting the boxes onto the small table, I turn and face Kinsley.

"What took me so long?" I reply sarcastically. "Well, let's start with the visitor who showed up at my door the moment I was getting out of the shower. Let's start there."

Kinsley looks at me and there's a small grin that stretches across her face.

"I don't know what you're talking about, but I'm glad to see you got the wine glasses and vases here for Ellie to see."

Looking over her shoulder, I see Ellie and Brea standing near a rack of dresses. Kinsley's grandma, June, is sitting in a chair off to the side. She smiles as she watches Ellie hold out each dress she browses.

With an annoyed smile on my face I nod my head. "Wouldn't want to ruin your plans," I retort, waving my hands at her and her notebook. She's been using that thing to call out orders to all of us for the past week. Strolling past Kinsley, I wrap my friend in a hug.

"You look so pretty, Ells. Are you excited to find the perfect dress?"

"Honestly, some of these dresses are so intimidating," she sighs. "I just want something simple. Callum promised me simple."

Ellie doesn't ask for a lot, but the one thing she did say was she wanted a small wedding. She wanted a day filled with all the people she loved as she tied the knot of forever with the only man she's ever loved. Callum, being Callum, promised to give her everything she ever wanted and more. He just wanted to know she was his.

I'm so happy to see someone who deserves it more than anyone finally get her day.

I can't deny the small part of me that feels my heart ache in my chest after seeing Graham today. Five years ago, I thought I found my forever. We were young but were so in love. The two of us together, I thought there was nothing in the world that could tear us apart.

Moments like this, the memories come crashing over me in waves. I find myself doing what I've always done to bury the pain, I find ways of coping, distracting me from the way my heart aches with missing him.

Bringing myself back to the present, I run my hand along Ellie's back before I whisper in her ear, "I promise it will be everything you want and more."

Standing back, I flash Ellie my best smile hoping that it hides my sadness and gives her the reassurance she needs.

"Why don't you show us one of the dresses you have your eye on? Do you have a style you had in mind?"

Kinsley start clapping her hands excitedly.

"Ells, I promise you're going to look stunning." Kinsley walks toward her, reaching over her shoulder to pull a dress off the rack. "I saw you looking at this one. I think you should try it on. Who knows, maybe this is THE dress!"

I take a seat next to June and she reaches over, patting my forearm. "Hi, sweetie, you doin' alright?"

Running my thumb over my fingernail, my mind wanders elsewhere. As soon as I hear the lock on the dressing room door, my eyes shoot up to find Ellie looking stunning in a gorgeous white dress.

It's simple and form-fitting, molding to her body like it was meant for her. Blush highlights her cheeks. She's never liked being the center of attention, but the sparkle in her eye shows just how happy she truly is.

Kinsley lifts the train behind her, using her other hand to help Ellie step onto the platform. We all turn to look in the mirror, searching for any sight of what Ellie may be thinking, but the subtle way she bites her lip shows she's trying to fight back the smile that wants to let loose on her face.

"Ellie, oh my God," Kinsley mutters, pressing her hand to her mouth as tears form in her eyes. I force down the emotion rising in my throat. She looks beautiful.

Ellie's had an incredibly hard life, facing more tragedy and heartbreak than any one person should ever have to endure. Nearly nine months ago, we almost lost her when she was assaulted and abducted. She's fought her way out of that life, and she continues to fight with every ounce of determination in her. No one in this world deserves the happiness she has been given more and seeing how happy she looks in that dress has tears silently streaming down my face.

"What do you think?" Brea asks. Looking around the room, I notice there isn't a dry eye in sight.

"I love it! It's pretty and so perfect. Do you think Callum would like it?"

Ellie bites the inside of her cheek, looking uncertain. There's a hesitancy in her voice, before Kinsley interrupts the seriousness of the moment bursting out laughing.

"Are you kidding? He's going to lose his shit when he sees you walking down the aisle and I can't wait to see it happen."

June laughs softly and I know she, along with the rest of us, agrees with Kinsley's statement. Although I'm positive Callum would be tripping over her no matter what dress she picked.

Ellie quickly swipes away the tear that threatens to fall before she subtlety nods her head agreeing. "I think this is the one then." She smiles. "Oh, God, I'm getting married."

She says the statement with shock underlying her tone, as if she can't believe it's about to happen either.

"You and Callum are going to live a happy life, Ells."

We snap a few pictures of her in the dress, being sure to capture different angles. Holding out my hand, I help her back to the fitting room to change.

Kinsley is back to work looking over the rack of bridesmaid's dresses, so I reassure her I'll help Ellie as she gets the rest of the dresses in order.

I feel her eyes are burning into me, as if she, too, is sensing something is wrong.

"You've been pretty quiet today. It's like your mind is somewhere else. How are you handling everything?" Ellie asks quietly.

"What do you mean?" I question, as she slides the dress down over her hips.

"Brea told us about Graham moving back to town. I figured the news would be hard on you. You don't have to pretend with me though, Halle. I'm here if you ever need to talk."

This is what I love most about Ellie. She's been through so much in her life that she understands the hard. When you need someone to be there for you, not necessarily with the right words to heal you, but just be there for you—it's her.

"I'm sorry, it seems selfish of me. I don't want today to be about me. This is such an incredibly exciting time for you. I promise I'll pull out of my funk. Seeing him earlier was unexpected and more difficult than I ever thought it would be."

"You don't have to worry about that with me, Halle. If there is anyone who understands how you're feeling, it's me. You don't have to pretend around me. Like I said, I'm here for you. You just let me know when you're ready."

I nod. "Thanks, babe." I give her a reassuring smile. She reaches out to grab my hand, squeezing it.

"Now seriously, let's talk about how Callum's going to react when he sees you in this dress. You'd look great in a potato sack, that's why I hate you. He's going to be crying, stumbling over his words. It's going to be adorable." I laugh.

She blushes, her smile growing a mile wide. "That's my plan."

I'd always hoped I'd see Graham again, but having it become reality has me lost in my head. Lost in the past, but I'm doing my best to pull myself out of it. I've been forcing a smile on my face for a long time. I've gotten somewhat good at it by now.

We all have that one person our hearts will always go running back to and, for me, that person will always be Graham. I only wish I were his reason to stay.

## Do you want more Graham and Halle?

Grab your copy of Until I Found You at:
www.authorbrookeobrien.com/untilifoundyo
u

# BOOKS BY BROOKE

*A Rebels Havoc Series*

Brix
Sins of a Rebel
Tysin
Trey
Madden

*Men of Blaze*

Personal Foul
Reckless Rebound (Cocky Hero Club)

*Tattered Heart Duet*

Torn
Tattered

*A Heart's Compass Series*

Where I Found You
Lost Before You
Until I Found You

Now That I Found You
Where You Belong

*Standalones (In order of publication)*

Wild Irish

**Learn more and purchase your copy at:**
www.authorbrookeobrien.com/booksby-
brooke

# PLAYLIST

Check out Brooke's writing inspiration, along with some of Mav & Ryan's favorites.

Scars – Papa Roach
Your Guardian Angel – Red Jumpsuit Apparatus
Only One – Yellowcard
Addicted – Saving Abel
Broken – Seether
Without You – Hinder
Life After You – Daughtry
Here Without You – 3 Doors Down
The Reason – Hoobastank
Second Chance – Shinedown
Alone – I Prevail

**Listen to the Playlist on Spotify at:**
www.authorbrookeobrien.com/tattered

# ABOUT BROOKE

USA Today Bestselling author Brooke O'Brien writes steamy and swoon-worthy new adult romances. She's best known for her sports and rock star romances.

Brooke believes a love worth having is worth fighting for, and she brings this into her stories where her characters risk it all for love.

When she isn't writing or falling in love with a new book boyfriend, you can find her spending time with her family, cheering on her favorite sports teams, listening to ASMR, or binge-watching the latest true crime documentary. She loves rockin' a comfy hoodie with leggings and believes the best days include a good nap.

Brooke loves connecting with readers and hopes you'll join her on her social pages or reader group to stay in touch. To follow Brooke and join her newsletter, visit authorbrookeobrien. com/follow.

# ACKNOWLEDGMENTS

I have so many people I want to thank for helping me on this amazing journey. I'm grateful beyond words for everyone who has been there for me, especially those who took a chance on me in the beginning.

Thank you to my amazing readers for picking up my books and taking a chance on my stories. To everyone who has left a review, sent me a message or a comment, THANK YOU! I can't even begin to tell you how happy it makes me when I hear from you.  To all the bloggers who support me and help spread the word of my releases, you matter! I couldn't do this without you and your love for books.

My Boys - Everything I do in this life is for you. I could never find the words to describe how much I love you.

Asha (a.k.a. Smash) - We've been through a lot together over the past few months, but I'm so grateful to have you as my sister bestie. Thanks for always being there for me, through the thick and thin. Love you!

To my AMAZING beta readers Giovanna, Julia, Erin and Ana - Thank you for sparing your time and reading Maverick and Ryan's story in the rawest form. You are always so honest with your feedback. I owe a big hug and a thank you to my editor, Rox LeBlanc, and my proofreader, Julie Deaton, for helping me polish off this story and making it the best it could be. I appreciate all of you for being patient with me on this one.

To Kate - Thank you so much for being there for me. We may not always talk everyday, but I hope you know how grateful I am to have you as my friend.

To Najla Qamber with Najla Qamber Designs - Thank you to you and your amazing team! You are so incredibly talented and always such a pleasure to work with. You put up with me and my numerous changes, but always end up blowing me away by bringing my vision to life.

# COPYRIGHT

Tattered: Tattered Heart Duet (#2)
Copyright © 2018 by Brooke O'Brien with Tattered Ink Publishing
All Rights Reserved

No part of this book may be reproduced or transmitted in any form or by any means, electronic or mechanical, including photocopying, recording, or by any information storage and retrieval system without written permissions of the author, except for the use of brief quotations in a review.

This is a work of fiction. Names, characters, and incidents either are the product of the author's imagination or are used fictitiously. Any resemblance to persons, living or dead, business establishments, events, or locales is entirely coincidental. The author acknowledges the trademarked status and trademark owners of various products referenced in this work of fiction, which has been used without permission. The publication/use of these trademarks is not authorized, associated with or sponsored by the trademark owners.

For information on subsidiary rights, please contact Tattered Ink Publishing at www.authorbrookeobrien.com.